MURDOCK'S LAW

MURDOCK'S LAW

LOREN D. ESTLEMAN

DOUBLEDAY & COMPANY, INC.
GARDEN CITY, NEW YORK
1982

Library of Congress Cataloging in Publication Data

Estleman, Loren D.
Murdock's law.

I. Title.
PS3555.S84M8   813'.54
AACR2
ISBN: 0-385-17957-X
Library of Congress Catalog Card Number 81-43410
Copyright © 1982 by Loren D. Estleman
All Rights Reserved
Printed in the United States of America
First Edition

MURDOCK'S LAW

CHAPTER 1

The hearse was drawn by a pair of arrogant-looking matched blacks with coats that shone like stretched satin, plumed bridles, and the general appearance of never having been whipped up above a trot. Black bunting framed the casket between the side windows, an expensive affair of polished mahogany with gold-plated handles under a mound of lilies and hyacinth. The driver, a square, rough-handed Irishman whose nose glowed redder than the early spring chill dictated, looked bored and thirsty. The fellow beside him, rotund in a black cutaway, striped trousers, and a high silk hat screwed down to the eyes, looked inconsolable. I took him for the undertaker. The richer they get the sadder they look.

There was a respectable procession behind, led by a gray-whiskered preacher and a stout, middle-aged woman weeping behind a black veil, but before they reached my end of the street I stepped inside to avoid having to doff my hat. After living in it for four days I wasn't so sure my scalp wouldn't peel off with it.

A bell mounted overhead jangled when I closed the door. Racks of rifles and shotguns lined the walls of the shop, their straight black barrels glistening smugly in the light streaming in through the big front window. Standing out from the walls, wooden-framed glass cases containing more firearms in various stages of assembly formed a square within a square. The place smelled sharply of lubricating oil.

Behind the cases, at a bench littered with springs and rags

and short screws and miscellaneous instruments, a scrawny old man was filing the rough edges off the inside of a rifle barrel clamped in a wooden vise. He said without turning that he'd be with me directly. His Swedish accent would sink a ferry.

"Who died?" I asked.

"Town marshal." The file rasped shrilly against the jagged steel.

"Shot?"

"Choked on a piece of steak."

I wondered if he was joking. He didn't strike me as the type. "That must have come as a surprise in this town. I hear folks around here raise some hell from time to time."

"From time to time."

"Not that I've seen any evidence of it."

He squatted to peer inside the barrel. His profile was clean but beginning to blur under the chin. He wore a massive blond moustache streaked with white that swept to the corners of his jaw and appeared to have sucked all the hair from the top of his bald head.

"What'd you expect, shooting?" he said then. "All day long, every day, like you read in the penny dreadfuls? There ain't that much lead in Montana." He blew through the barrel and scraped a thick finger around inside. Apparently satisfied, he straightened and turned to face me. His gray-blue eyes took me in swiftly from dusty crown to caked spurs. "What's your business?"

"Page Murdock. I wired you last week from Helena looking for a Deane-Adams. You said you had one."

"Hell of a long ride just for a gun."

"I was coming anyway."

His eyes narrowed. "You some kind of law?"

"Does it show?"

"You could be on one side or the other, from the look of you. In this business I see my share of both."

2

"Maybe you've seen Chris Shedwell lately," I said. "My boss got a report he's on his way here. He's wanted for a mail-train robbery near Wichita two years ago."

He shook his head. "Thought you boys favored those." He indicated the Army Colt in my holster. "Deane-Adams only shoots five."

"I know. I used to own one."

"You only got four if you keep the chamber under the hammer empty," he pointed out.

"I don't."

"Shoot your foot off someday." He drew a ring of keys from his pocket and bent to unlock a drawer in the bottom of the case between us. From its depths he lifted a skeletal piece and handed it to me.

It was a slim, lightweight .45 with an octagonal barrel, a smooth cylinder, and a skinny butt showing no more curve than a spinster's bodice. It looked exactly like the one I had lost the year before somewhere on the tracks between Fargo and Bismarck, except that this one had a mother-of-pearl grip.

"Who ruined it?" I asked.

"Tinhorn from Minnesota. He won it at stud and paid me to fit the new grip. Never picked it up. Miner caught him shaving the ace of clubs and carved him up with a pocket-knife. They buried him in pieces."

"How soon can I have it refitted?"

"Tomorrow. Be twenty dollars for the gun and the work. Half in advance."

I gave him ten and got a receipt.

After the comparative silence of the shop, the noise on the street was terrific. Once a mining town, Breen had died when the vein east of the Smith River played out, only to be born again as the cattle industry stretched into the foothills between the Big and Little Belt Mountains. Merchants had swarmed in armed with canned goods and coal oil and curtain material and all the other paraphernalia of eastern culture,

3

just as they had in countless other boomtowns across the Northwest in the eighteen-seventies, so that you couldn't tell Helena from Sutter's Mill, Bismarck from Dodge. I washed the taste of civilization out of my mouth in one of fourteen saloons that faced each other across a street as wide as a pasture and got directions to the marshal's office.

It was a solid affair built of logs, with weatherboard on the outside to give visitors the impression that it wasn't. A square of brown butcher paper was nailed to the door with GONE TO THE FUNERAL penciled across it in an educated hand. I waited.

After ten minutes or so a lean twist of hide in a frock coat and striped trousers strode down the boardwalk with a key in his hand. The face under a round-brimmed Spanish hat was leathern, cracked at the corners of the eyes and stretched taut across a very straight nose that came almost to a point. He wore a drooping black moustache and a gold star the size of a tea saucer attached by tiny gold chains to a nameplate on his vest. The nameplate was blank, but the words "City Marshal, Breen, M.T." were engraved on the star in the center of a lot of scrollwork.

I said, "You must be the new city marshal."

He stopped short, fingers dangling near the ivory butt of a Navy Colt on his right hip. I have that effect on people.

"You have the advantage." His voice was thin and tight, like everything else about him.

I gave him my name and got out the simple star that said DEPUTY U.S. MARSHAL, no chains or scrollwork. "It's not as nice as yours."

"You're the one wired Bram about Shedwell coming," he said.

"Bram?"

"Abraham Arno." He sounded like a schoolmaster prompting a slow pupil. "We just put him in a hole north of town."

"Did he really choke on a piece of steak?"

"That's what his widow says. I think she poisoned him, but

4

that's only the opinion of a temporary marshal." He unlocked the door and went inside, leaving it open. I closed it behind me.

There was clapboard on the inside, whitewashed and broken up only by the stovepipe, a gun rack, a single barred window looking out on the dusty street, and a sheaf of wanted dodgers tacked to the wall behind the desk, brown and curling. A partition across the back partially screened a row of unoccupied cells beyond. Over everything hung a heavy odor of boiled coffee and cigars.

"You ride for Judge Blackthorne." He pegged his hat next to the door, passed through a gate in an oak railing, and took a seat in a wooden swivel behind the desk. He looked younger with his abundance of black hair exposed, somewhere in his late twenties. "I hear when folks in Helena get bored they stick him in a pit with a grizzly just to see fur fly."

"That's him. What about Shedwell?"

He slipped an ivory comb from the inside breast pocket of his coat and glided it through his pompadour. I watched him wipe bay rum off the teeth with a red silk handkerchief before putting it away and calculated the depth of my dislike for him.

"No sign of him yet," he said. "I think someone was having fun with your boss."

"That'll be the day. Are you as much law as they got around here?"

He lost his good nature. His eyes were murky pools of no color you could put a name to. "You ride a fast mouth for one man."

"They give you deputies?"

It took him a moment to answer. His eyes never moved. "Two full-time. And the geezer that watches the place when there are prisoners. Why?"

"They all been looking for Shedwell?"

"They're deputies, aren't they?"

"Do they even know what he looks like? Do you?" When he didn't answer, I pulled out the soggy reader I'd had plastered to my chest for fifty miles and peeled it open under his nose. It featured a fair likeness of the man I was after from his night-riding days, under a line offering a thousand dollars for his capture. The marshal studied it a moment, then leaned back, squeaking his chair.

"Haven't seen him."

"He was pretty fresh when this was done," I pressed. "He's aged some since."

He shook his head. His expression was condescending. I said, "What do they call you?"

"Yardlinger. Oren Yardlinger."

I blinked. "And you let them?"

"What the hell's that supposed to mean?" Pale slashes showed on his cheeks like healed-over scars.

I placed the paper on his blotter. "Tack it up. Have your men look at it and let me know if he shows. I'll be around."

"Why should he?" Something of his normal color had returned. "I hear he's selling his gun these days. There's no business for him here."

"How many men did you bury last month?"

"Six, but what's that got to do with anything?"

"How many of them died in bed?"

"One." He hesitated. "He held on for two weeks after a crazy half-breed split his skull with an oak chair over at the Glory."

I tapped the bulletin I'd given him. "When you've got something you'll find me at the Freestone Inn. Room twelve."

I'd dropped my valise off at the hotel on my way into town. Returning, I got out my city clothes and a razor and went down to the bathhouse, where I spent a leisurely half hour scraping off the trail dust and the worst of my whiskers. Afterward I left my riding clothes to be laundered and mounted the stairs to my room, drowsiness spreading through me like

6

the warmth from a shot of whiskey. But in the carpeted hallway outside I stopped.

You start to develop a sixth sense after you've been on the
frontier a while. Camping in the desert, you know before you
pull your boots on that there's a scorpion curled up in one of
them. Riding along the trail, you feel a road agent waiting for
you around the next bend. Those who didn't learn to detect
the unseen signs of danger didn't last long enough to unpack
their bags. That was how I was sure without opening the door
that there was someone in my room.

And since whoever it was hadn't bothered to ask my leave,
I could only assume that he felt it wouldn't matter much
longer.

CHAPTER 2

Once in Missoula I had waited outside a cabin for two and a half hours until the killer who was laying for me got impatient and tried to shoot his way out. I put three slugs in him sight unseen before he reached the door. I could have played it that way this time, except that I was too tired for stealth and too mad to give whoever it was the satisfaction. Instead I kicked the door open and dived in headfirst, sliding on my stomach with my Colt clasped in front of me in both hands. I interrupted a game of solitaire on the bed.

The player, seated on the edge of the mattress, was thin in a sickly sort of way, with pinched shoulders and a sunken chest and hollows in his cheeks that were accentuated by the curve of his reddish side-whiskers. Startled, he dropped the deck and swept aside the skirt of his Prince Albert to get at a small pistol stuck in his waistband.

"Call!" I shouted.

He froze with his hand on the curved butt. I could hear his labored breathing. Slowly he raised his hands to shoulder level.

There was another man standing next to the window, but his hands were empty and clear of his body. For what seemed a long time I lay motionless, the .44 cocked and commanding the middle ground between the two, before the thin man spoke. He had the kind of voice that made you want to clear your throat.

9

"You always come into a room like that, or is this a special occasion?"

"It varies with my mood." I got up, keeping them both covered. "Do you always break into other people's rooms just to play cards?"

"No one broke anything," he said. "The clerk let us in while you were bathing."

"Nice town. The merchants and the burglars work together. Who goes to jail, the marshal?"

"The responsibility is mine."

I studied the man at the window. He was small, not much larger than a twelve-year-old boy, but with a large head, and looked so dapper in spats, striped trousers, and a black coat with a pinched waist that I was reminded of a poster I had seen of General Tom Thumb in full uniform standing in the palm of a man's hand. His black hair was combed into a fussy lock on his forehead, which, together with his spadelike chin whiskers and moustache waxed into points, turned him into a junior-size Napoleon III. He had liquid brown eyes.

"I persuaded the clerk to allow us to wait for you in your quarters." His French accent was guttural. "It was unseemly for men of our reputation to be seen standing about a hotel lobby. We have tampered with none of your things."

I said, "Who are you? Just so I can introduce you to Marshal Yardlinger when we get to the jail."

The thin man chuckled dryly. I glared at him and he fell silent.

"I am Michel d'Oléron, Marquis de Périgueux," the little man replied, bowing his head slightly and exposing a bald spot like a monk's tonsure. "You may call me Périgueux if you wish."

"I'll think about it."

He turned his palm upward, indicating his partner. "The gentleman you found too slow with the firearm is Dick Mather, owner of the Six Bar Six, across which you doubtless rode on your way to Breen. We are both ranchers. As of last month, I control something over two million acres of grassland between Monsieur Mather's property and the Big Horn Mountains in Wyoming Territory."

"That's a bite to chew for someone from Europe," I said.

He smiled complacently without showing teeth. "It is larger than Corsica and Sardinia combined."

"Thanks. Now that I've had my geography lesson, I'd appreciate it if you and Dick would pile all your excess iron on the floor at the foot of the bed."

"But of course. Monsieur?"

Carefully, the emaciated one the Frenchman called Mather drew the derringer from his waistband, got up to place it on the floral carpet, and backed away. I looked at Périgueux.

"I am unarmed, monsieur. *Voilà*." He unbuttoned and swung open his coat. His vest was yellow silk, with an ornament of red and gold dangling from one pocket.

"Nice fob," I said.

He fondled it. "It was presented to me by the late emperor. Unfortunately, military medals have no place in civil life, and so it must serve the purpose of assisting me in learning the time of day. It is all I have left to remind me of a glorious era."

"Show me the watch."

He raised his eyebrows. There were traces of gray in them, like dust in snuff. I explained.

"I cornered a rapist in Deer Lodge a couple of years ago who had a derringer attached to a fob like that one. I'm still carrying the ball."

With a continental shrug, he reached two fingers into the pocket and produced an ornate gold watch with a capital N engraved on the lid, encircled by oak leaves. I nodded. He replaced it.

"You and Louis Napoleon must have been pretty tight."

"I was a marshal of France."

11

"I didn't think the nobility got along with the Bonapartes."

"It is to them that I owe my title. It was bestowed upon me along with certain lands when I married into the family."

"Cozy."

"*Pardon?*"

I shook my head and put up the Colt to retrieve Mather's gun from the floor. Unloading it, I placed the cartridges on the writing desk next to the door and returned the piece to its owner. "Now, let's all have a seat and discuss why I shouldn't turn you over to the marshal."

"To begin with," growled Mather, "the marshal takes his orders from us."

I scaled my hat onto the bed and leaned back against the desk. Périgueux had claimed the room's only upholstered chair, while Mather had resumed his perch on the edge of the bed.

"Isn't that the city council's responsibility?" I asked.

"Indeed," responded the Frenchman. "In addition to the Six Bar Six, Monsieur Mather maintains controlling interest in two local saloons, which qualifies him for his elected position on the council. I hold no property in Breen. To do so would be just a formality in any case, since I am now the largest rancher in Montana and my word alone carries certain weight."

Mather was growing impatient. Two feverish spots of red the size of half-dollars showed high on his cheeks. Together with his otherwise sallow complexion and wasted frame, they branded him a consumptive. "Oh, get on with it, Mike!" He nailed me with glistening eyes. "We understand you're a United States marshal."

"Deputy," I corrected. "Yardlinger didn't waste any time spreading the word around, did he?"

"It was not he who told us," interjected Périgueux. "He mentioned it to one of his deputies, who got word to me at the Breen House, where I am staying on business. I decided to send a messenger for Monsieur Mather."

"All that for little me," I said.

"Yes." If the Frenchman had picked up on the sarcasm, he didn't respond to it. "Ever since Marshal Arno's death two days ago we have been discussing what steps we can take to alleviate the current situation, and it would appear that your arrival is most timely. To be succinct—"

"Too late."

Again he ignored my bad manners. "We wish to engage your services."

"We need a town marshal," Mather said.

"What's wrong with Yardlinger?"

"Monsieur Yardlinger," said the Frenchman, "is a boy. His experience—"

"There are no boys west of the Mississippi."

Périgueux looked patient. "Yes, we are familiar with your frontier slogans. The fact remains that his experience has not prepared him for the duties of a man in his position. This is not true in your case. Your reputation, Monsieur Murdock, precedes you."

I used a word I'd learned long ago in the cavalry. Even Périgueux was taken aback. "I do not understand."

"I don't know how to say it in French," I replied. "So far I haven't heard anything to change my mind about placing both of you under arrest. Why don't you start by telling me what's coming up that you'd rather I didn't know about until I'm pinned to that pretty gold badge."

"You see?" Mather told the Frenchman. "We should have come right out with it at the beginning, like I said."

The Marquis sighed. Why did I have the feeling I was watching a carefully rehearsed play?

"It is not really much of a revelation, since you have been inquiring around about it before this," he said. "You know

13

that a certain man, a certain gunman, is expected here shortly."

"Shedwell."

"Yes. But you do not know why, and neither do we. For some weeks past, there have been difficulties here. Perhaps you have heard something of them in Helena."

"Range war," I acknowledged.

"Yes, but only a little one." He emphasized how little with his thumb and forefinger. "The small ranchers, they are jealous of the big ranchers and the grass and water we control. Until now the situation has been of small consequence—a fight with the fists between cowboys from different spreads, an occasional bullet through a window, aimed high so that no one is hurt. The presence of a hired killer, however, changes everything."

"Who's hiring him?"

He spread his delicate hands, hunching his shoulders at the same time in a Latin show of befuddlement. "Your guess is equal to mine, monsieur. Certainly not we. We have our suspicions, of course."

"I'll bet you do."

Mather said, "We can't have this kind of thing happening. If the small ranchers start hiring iron we'll have to retaliate, and then we've got a full-scale war on our hands. The next thing you know, the army will step in like they did in Lincoln County, and then everybody loses."

"What do you want me to do? I'm planning to arrest Shedwell anyway."

"That is precisely what we do not want," spoke up Périgueux. "These small fry, as I believe they are sometimes called, crave a lesson in competition. As a servant of the federal government, your duty is simply to take him into custody. As city marshal and keeper of the local peace, you would be expected to deliver a somewhat more stringent message to those who would endanger it."

14

I invested the better part of a minute picking apart his speech and turning the pieces over in my head before I grinned and said, "Mr. Marquis—"

"Please. Périgueux."

"That's got to be the politest way anyone ever tried to hire someone else to kill a man."

The mood in the room changed, grew lighter. The pair exchanged triumphant looks. Said the Frenchman: "Then may we assume that we have reached accord?"

"You may assume that if you aren't out of this room in two minutes I'll pump you both so full of lead you'll reach the lobby without using the stairs."

There was a very long pause. It might have gone even longer had not someone knocked at the door. I looked questioningly at Périgueux, who shook his head stiffly. His face had turned the color of old blood. I called out to the visitor to identify himself.

"Messenger, sir," came the muffled reply from the hallway. "Telegram for Deputy Murdock."

Some more time went by. I was still looking at the Marquis. "If he has anything in his hand besides a telegram, you'll get the answer quicker than anything Western Union ever delivered."

I drew the Colt and sidled up to the door, opening it at arm's length with my back to the wall. A boy in worn overalls leaned in to stare at me around the jamb. He was holding an envelope and nothing else. I holstered the gun to accept it and gave him too much money to make up for feeling like a jackass.

"I had to make sure no accidents were arranged in case I turned you down," I told the ranchers, after the boy had gone. I tore open the envelope. The wire was brief, the way the Judge liked them.

HAVE BEEN NOTIFIED DEATH MARSHAL ARNO STOP

YOU WILL PERFORM DUTIES HIS OFFICE UNTIL PER-
MANENT REPLACEMENT SELECTED

                              HARLAN BLACKTHORNE

I met Périgueux's gaze above the margin. He read the gist
of the message in my expression.

"We took the liberty of wiring your superior before coming
here," he explained. "We had no idea at the time that you
would react so strongly to our little proposition. You will dis-
regard the directive, of course." He got up and retrieved a
malacca stick from the corner next to the window. "Monsieur
Mather?"

"Just a minute," I said. "Where do I go to get sworn in?"

Mather's narrow face grew blotchy again. Périgueux studied me closely, his disproportionately large head tilted back to
peer up at me.

"Your jest goes unappreciated." He forgot to say "monsieur."

"The gentle folk call me a maverick," I explained. "It's a
polite way of saying I don't know who my father is. Rules are
not something I pay a great deal of attention to. But I'm not
thickheaded enough to ignore a direct order, especially not
when it's in writing." I rattled the paper.

Mather called me a name I'd heard before. The Frenchman
fingered the head of his stick.

"We shall of course take steps to have the order rescinded."

"Dandy. When it is, you'll find me down at the jailhouse." I
opened the door for him.

His expression was hard to read. "May I remind you that
you are no longer in the territorial capital and that out here
the people have learned to make do with their own version of
the law."

"Long live the republic," I said. Neither of my guests
seemed impressed on their way out.

CHAPTER 3

After they left, I gazed longingly at the bed for a few seconds, then retrieved my hat and followed them out. I had three hours of daylight left and too much to do to spend them between sheets, even if they were the first sheets I'd seen in days.

Yardlinger was poking a fresh chunk of maple into the stove when I entered the marshal's office. A heavy-shouldered farm boy in overalls and a burlap-brown suit coat was reading a yellowback novel in a chair behind the railing. He marked his place with a dirty forefinger and studied me through suspicious blue eyes. His hair was corn-yellow, and a sparse sprouting of the same color glittered along his upper lip. He wore a plain star pinned to one overall strap.

"No Shedwell yet," announced the other, swinging shut the stove lid with a squeal of rusted hinges.

"I'm replacing you as marshal."

Some kinds of news are best sprung right away, with no waltzing. This wasn't one of them, but I was tired and didn't have a lot of time. Some of the murkiness had gone out of his gaze as he turned it on me.

"Who says?"

"Western Union." I extended the telegram. He hesitated before accepting it, as if that meant surrender. It struck me, as he read, that his paperwork had doubled since I had come to town. He went through it again, more slowly the second time, then refolded it and put it in his inside breast pocket.

"I'll have to confirm this."

"I thought you would," I said.

"You want him out of here, Oren?"

We both looked at the towheaded deputy, who had risen from his seat and slipped a hamlike hand into the right side pocket of his threadbare coat. He was two inches taller than I and a dozen pounds heavier, which didn't concern me. The lump in his coat pocket did.

"All right, you've stood by your boss," I said. "Now put the gun down on the railing and let the grown-ups finish their business."

"You talk tall for a dead man." He was quivering all over.

"So do you."

His brow knitted, and then he looked at my right hand. I had the Colt pressed to my hip and pointing at his navel.

"How the hell—"

"Experience. Empty that pocket or I'll paint you all over the wall."

"Do what he says, Earl," Yardlinger counseled.

The gun was a Smith & Wesson pocket model .38, good enough for indoor shooting, which was the kind lawmen usually had to deal with. When it was on the railing and he had moved beyond reach of it, Earl looked even younger, nineteen at the outside.

"Go home and get some sleep," the erstwhile marshal told him. "You'll be needed tonight when those rannies from the Six Bar Six start showing up."

"You ain't going to just let him take over!"

"Go *home*, Earl!" Yardlinger's voice was higher and thinner than usual. The deputy reddened around the ears and banged through the gate, trailing muttered barnyard expletives into the street.

I holstered the Colt. It hadn't been fired except for practice since I'd bought it to replace the lost Deane-Adams, but all this leathering and unleathering was going to wear it out. "Did you tell him about me?" I asked Yardlinger.

"Why?" He produced a long cheroot from the pocket containing the telegram I'd given him and struck a match on the stove, just to give himself something to do. He had quick, nervous fingers, lean like the rest of him and callused.

"One of your deputies told Périgueux I was in town." I told him about our meeting.

The former marshal finished lighting the cheroot and held up the match, watching the flame burn down to within an eighth of an inch of his thumb and forefinger before he blew it out. It seemed to calm him.

"They were all here when I brought up the subject," he said. "I told them to keep an eye on you. That was when I was still employed." He started to undo the splendid badge.

"Hold onto it. You'll just have to put it back on when Périgueux gets through wiring my boss about what a menace I am to the community."

"I never keep anything no one wants me to have." The scrap of metal clattered onto the desk.

"Pin on a regular star then. I need deputies."

He hesitated. "I didn't think you liked me. Besides, you don't wear one."

"They put holes in your shirt, most of them from bullets. And I haven't met anyone I liked since I came to this town."

I watched him lean across the desk and open a drawer from which he plucked an unmarked six-pointer like the one Earl wore. He wiped it off on his sleeve and put it on.

"I wouldn't be doing this except that I don't ever want to smell another cow close up," he explained.

I'd handled cattle too before turning to the law. I was beginning to like him in spite of myself. Brusquely I said, "This thing about deputies carrying tales bothers me. Did any of them leave the office within a half hour after you told them I was in town?"

19

"I couldn't say. I left right after to grab a bite. I put Randy Cross in charge. He's my—your other full-time deputy. You just met Earl Trotter. That leaves Major Brody, the old-timer who fills in as jailer when the rest of us are busy. He just stopped by to kill some time. Any one of them could have done it."

"Who would you suspect?"

"None." He smoked and brooded. "At least we know it wasn't Earl. You saw how much he thinks of your taking my place."

"I saw what he wanted me to see. That puts him at the top of my list."

"Well, you'll meet them all soon enough. That's your worry now. I don't suppose you want to tell me why it's so important for Périgueux and Mather to have a spy in this office, or why they're so het up to have you here."

"Were," I corrected. "I told you, they're worried about Chris Shedwell. They didn't hire him, so they figure the other ranchers did. They looked at my background and thought I'd be a good one to fire the last shot Shedwell ever hears. Sort of a noisy object lesson."

Yardlinger's cheeks paled slightly, a dangerous sign. "So here you are," he said. "A hired killer who carries a badge."

"I didn't say I took them up on the offer. You've got the reason I'm here in your pocket. They like me even less than you do right now."

He continued to stare at me. After a long time he nodded jerkily. "I'll believe that. Right up until you kill Shedwell or he kills you. Either way you die."

"I think your fire's gone out."

I indicated the stove. The cheery glow had faded from the space where the hinged lid didn't quite fit the opening. Clamping the half-smoked cheroot between his teeth, he yanked open the lid, worked the damper, and blew and stirred the embers until a flame appeared.

"What's the problem with the men from the Six Bar Six?" I asked.

"Hm?" He was watching the blaze creep along the edge of the split maple. It burned blue in the center.

"You told Earl you'd need him when those rannies from the Six Bar Six showed up. That's Dick Mather's spread, isn't it?"

He nodded, closing the lid. "He's got a lot of hotheads slapping his brand this year. A bunch from Bob Terwilliger's ranch east of here is staying in town and there might be trouble." He snorted. "There *will* be trouble. Mather's been accusing Terwilliger of cutting out Six Bar Six strays for months."

"Has he been rustling them?"

"Hell, you know these cowboys. Of course he has. But no one ever paid much attention to it. Until now."

"Is it just Terwilliger?"

"Probably not. He's kind of the unofficial head of the small ranchers around the territory, and none of them has enough respect for the big runners to fill a busted bushel basket, especially not for the Marquis. Folks around here generally tolerate foreigners until they start swallowing land like it's sugarcoated."

"Doesn't sound like you admire him much yourself."

His smoke didn't taste so good any more. He made a face and opened the stove to dispose of the stub. "Let's just say I don't have much use for rich people safe in Europe getting hold of the water rights over here and using them to control a hundred times more pasture than they own."

"I've seen it before," I said. "The rustling's an excuse for Périgueux and Mather to run the small fry out and claim their spreads. I take it there's been trouble already."

"Night riders. Grown men with pillowcases over their heads who gallop in and kidnap ranchers out of their beds and dump them out on the prairie to walk back ten miles naked. Last week they caught one of Terwilliger's hired hands on his way back to the bunkhouse and made out like they were going to lynch him to a dead oak."

He had been watching the fire. Now he twisted shut the damper and replaced the lid with more clang than was necessary.

"How'd you like to be set on your horse in the dark with your hands trussed behind you and a rope around your neck so tight you can't swallow, one slap away from a slow strangle? Yeah, they had a high old time that night. So high that when they finally untied him and let him go he just kept on riding until Terwilliger's son caught up with him to ask why he was stealing one of his father's horses, and the hand blurted out the story. He was so scared he'd soiled himself."

"You favor Terwilliger."

"I favor a man's right to do his job without having to hunch up every time he hears hoofbeats. Terwilliger's contributed his share to that feeling. He's offering a bonus to the first hand that brings back an ear belonging to a Six Bar Six man. Along about midnight, when every cowboy in town's had his fill of liquor, someone's going to try and collect that bounty. And that's why I told Earl he'd be needed."

"I hope you told the others the same thing. Those loaded?" I nodded at the rifles and shotguns in the rack behind the desk, chained together like convicts on a work detail.

"Every last one of them. Think we'll need them tonight?"

"Maybe not for shooting, but five men in badges standing around with long guns don't do much for a cowhand's fighting spirit. I'll need a key."

"Take mine." He pulled a ring out of his hip pocket.

"Keep it. They have a habit of getting lost just when you need them most. Did Arno have a separate key?"

"Up at the Breen House. He lived there the past year or so to get away from his wife. Room seven."

I'd seen the Breen on my way in. Four stories, with a restaurant on the ground floor and colored glass out front. I whistled. "What do you folks pay your marshals?"

"Forty a month and ten cents for every stray dog he shoots in the city limits."

"He must have shot a lot of dogs to afford a room in that hotel. Or that fancy box they planted him in."

When he scowled, the tips of his black moustache almost touched beneath his lower lip. "It helps to claim a cut of the profits of every game in town."

"I figured as much. His stuff still in the room?"

"Most of it. I packed up his clothes and sent them over to his widow. The rest is going to take some time. He was long on taking and short on giving away."

"I'll fetch the key. Get word to all the deputies I want to see them here in half an hour." I started for the door.

"All of them?" he called after me. "Even the Major? Hell, he's just—"

"All of them." The door swung shut on the end of it.

The Breen's lobby was carpeted in green plush with petit-pointed leaves and lit by a crystal chandelier whose journey around the Horn had me beat by twelve thousand miles. I'd seen bigger places, but they didn't have walls around them. The desk clerk wore a waxed moustache and parted his hair in the middle. He didn't want to give me the key to Room 7 even after I'd showed him my badge. He changed his mind after I grabbed a handful of his cravat and prepared to pin it to his tonsils. I left him repairing his haberdashery and mounted a broad, curving staircase clothed in more leafy green.

The room was three times the size of the one I was staying in at the Freestone. It too was carpeted, and ringed with marble-topped tables and chests of drawers covered in brocade and supporting most of the doodads a nineteenth-century gentleman required to survive socially. The bed was shiny brass and required a stepping stool to get into it from either side. A pair of double doors on my right suggested a closet. I had just started my search for the key to the gun rack when the room swelled with a tremendous explosion and I went down hard.

CHAPTER 4

The noise whistled in my ears for a time after I flattened out on my stomach, a position I was beginning to get used to. Pistols are noisy things outdoors; inside they're skull-rattlers. The air was hazy blue and stank of rotten eggs. I felt something on my back and knew that it was a litter of shattered glass from the mirror of the dressing table. An inch and a half to the right and I wouldn't have been feeling much of anything.

It may have been that my hearing was still affected or that my assailant was lighter on his feet than a prairie antelope, but I lay without moving for what seemed a long time before a shard of glass crunched not four feet back of my left ear. There was another long silence, and then I heard an almost inaudible rustle, as of clothing brushing against furniture. I heard it again a moment later, nearer, much nearer. Then silence again.

My heart was bounding between my ribs and the floor. I hoped whoever was in the room with me couldn't hear it. I kept my eyes open, concentrating my vision on a bit of gray lint on the carpet two inches in front of me to give them that glazed, motionless look. They burned in their sockets. I was working so hard on not blinking that I wasn't sure when the shadowy shape crept into the extreme corner of my range. Half a heartbeat later a shoe appeared beside me.

A woman's shoe.

It was expensive footwear, with a black patent-leather toe and an ivory top fastened with matching buttons. Above that

was a trim ankle in a black stocking and six or seven petticoats under a gray taffeta skirt, gathered up to keep them
from scuffing the floor. It was as tempting a target as had
been presented to me since the day Judge Blackthorne entered his chambers wearing a brand new beaver hat as tall as
a riding boot. I snatched the ankle in one hand and yanked.

She went down in an explosion of petticoats. More glass
shook loose from the dressing-table mirror. Something tipped
off the marble top, struck me between the shoulder blades
and rolled off. I ignored it. Still grasping her ankle, I threw
myself up onto my knees and forward, sprawling on top of
her. I'll try to report the rest in order.

She tried to bring a knee up into my crotch but missed, the
blow glancing off my left hip. Something flashed in her right
hand and I grabbed for it, but I misjudged and the something
banged the back of my skull. My hat had slipped to cushion
the blow, and her aim was off anyway; still, I had to fight
back nausea and unconsciousness to get my hands around her
flailing wrist. She raked my cheek with the nails of her free
hand. I cursed through my teeth and concentrated on gaining
possession of the gun. She bit my hand, took aim at my groin
again with her knee, and connected this time. The bottom
dropped out of my stomach, but before the real pain started I
threw a left hook at her jaw and she went limp.

By this time my insides were roiling. I started to climb off
her and noticed for the first time that we had attracted an audience. A group of people whom I took to be guests were
standing in the open doorway behind the prissy clerk, who
had tucked his cravat and collar back into place and was staring down at us the way I suppose desk clerks everywhere
stare down at men and women locked in mortal combat on
hotel room floors. I drew my Colt.

"Get the hell out of here."

I don't know if it was the gun, or the look on my face, or
the authoritative croak in which the command was delivered,

but it worked. He backed out, herding everyone with him, and pulled the door shut.

My opponent was still out. When the first wave of nausea had passed I stashed the Colt, scooped her gun out of her hand—it was a Smith pocket .32, smaller in caliber and more streamlined than the S&W carried by Yardlinger's young deputy—and stuck it in my belt. I got up and spent a few minutes with my hands on my knees, breathing deeply and waiting for the agony to move up and out. When it had, I attended to the other pains.

There was a knot the size of a quarter on the back of my skull. It was tender but the skin wasn't broken. With the scratches I wasn't so fortunate; I touched the stinging cheek and my fingers came back bloody. My handkerchief was soaked by the time the leaking stopped. By contrast my sparring partner, whom I had to all intents and purposes vanquished, had only a purple-black smear on the side of her jaw to show for our introduction. It hardly seemed fair.

Aside from that, it was an attractive face, if you liked them unconscious. She had a high white brow and eyes with long lashes, set a little too far apart, but from there down I couldn't fault it. The nose was unremarkable, the jawline delicate-looking but strong (I'd confirmed that), and she had the broad mouth then out of fashion but more suited to her than the popular Cupid's pout. Her hair was auburn and a litter of pins around her head said that she usually wore it up. She had a decent shape if you could trust first impressions in those days of whalebone and wire.

The struggle had disarranged her skirt and petticoats, exposing three inches of creamy thigh over the top of her right stocking.

One of the closet doors stood open and a woman's handbag lay on the floor inside. I picked it up. Inside I found the usual feminine accessories, among them a lace handkerchief embroidered with the initials C.B. in silver thread and a milliner's receipt for fifteen dollars made out to Colleen Bower. A stiff leather holster, decidedly unfeminine, was stitched to the bag's lining. I tried the Smith & Wesson in the holster. Perfect fit. I left it there and put the purse on a lamp table next to the closet.

The woman on the floor moaned and began to stir, showing more flesh above the stocking. As luck would have it, she came to just as I was covering it.

"I guess you don't like them moving," she said.

She had opened her eyes without any of the preliminaries and sat up, catching me in the act. They were nice eyes, pale blue with gold flecks in them. At the moment they were accusing.

"I only beat women," I rejoined. "I don't ravish them."

She flushed from hairline to bodice. "You'll excuse me if I don't take you at your word." Savagely she readjusted the skirt, concealing everything to the tops of her shoes. Then she put a hand to her bruised jaw.

"I don't usually hit ladies unless they try to kill me first." I tossed her the federal star. She caught it in one hand—surprising me for the third time since we'd met—glanced at it, and flipped it back. I had to clap it against my chest with both hands. This round was hers.

"Does a name go with it?"

"Sometimes," I said. "Not always. It's the kind of information bushwhackers have to earn. You can start by telling me what you've got against me breathing."

"If I'd wanted to kill you, we wouldn't be talking. I'm a fair shot with a pocket pistol." She glanced around for it halfheartedly, then gave up. "When I heard the key in the door I thought you were the desk clerk or Yardlinger come to take away some more of Bram's things, so I hid in the closet. I opened the door a crack, saw you searching the room, and thought you were one of those ghouls that read the obituary column and then rob dead men the day of their funerals. I

28

wanted to put a scare in you. Only you don't scare." She rubbed her jaw. "Did you have to hit so hard?"

"Probably not, but it felt good. You're Colleen Bower?"

Her eyes widened slightly, then shifted to the floor of the closet and wandered until they found her handbag on the lamp table. Her smile was rueful. "You're law, all right. Yes."

"How'd you get in?"

She reached inside her bodice and produced a key identical to the one I'd extorted from the clerk. "Bram gave it to me. Marshal Arno."

"I'm beginning to understand," I said.

"Bright fellow."

"What were you doing here?"

"I came to get something. May I stand?"

I nodded. She wobbled to her feet, found her balance, then brushed the dust and pieces of glass off her skirt and crossed unsteadily to a tall chest of drawers next to the bed. From the top drawer she took an ornate wooden jewelry box and opened it for my inspection. Its contents sparkled in the sunlight slanting in through the window overlooking the main drag.

"Pretty," I said.

"Bram sent all the way to New York for them. Of course, I couldn't wear them anywhere but in this room or there'd be talk. So we kept them here."

"That's like owning a fancy buggy and never taking it out of the stable."

"You're not telling me anything I don't know. But they're mine and I'm taking them with me."

"Guess again. How do I know he bought those baubles for you? Maybe they belong to his widow."

"That witch!" she spat. "They didn't even live together. He only went home to eat, which is why he's dead. If she didn't poison him, I didn't graduate at the head of my class from Miss Jessup's School for Genteel Young Ladies. Anyway, what business is it of yours who takes them? What federal law am I violating?"

"None that I know of. But as of an hour and a half ago I'm Marshal Arno's replacement." I told her my name. Her lips curled mockingly.

"Page Murdock. It sounds chivalric, like Childe Harold. Do you rescue damsels from dragons?"

"No, I generally knock them cold and have my way with them. The box." I held out my hand. She hesitated, then snapped shut the lid of the fancy case and surrendered it.

"If your story checks out I'll give it back," I said.

"It won't. The jewelry wasn't in my name and no one knew about them but Bram and me."

"That simplifies things. I'll hold onto them, and if no one asks about them, I'll know you're telling the truth."

"How do I know you won't just keep them?"

"Because I'm telling you I won't." I tucked the box under one arm. "Now I have to ask myself what I'll do with you. So far I've only your word that an arrangement existed between you and the late lamented peace officer of Breen. I know from experience that getting a key to this room is no problem."

"Ask around." Her smile remained mocking. "Don't confuse discretion with secrecy. Out here everyone knows everyone else's business. We just didn't parade it around or we would both have been run out of town on a rail. I've come close to that in other towns and it's not pleasant. Ask anyone how it was between us. Ask them."

While she was speaking, the door flew open and Oren Yardlinger spilled in, accompanied by the hotel clerk and three armed men. One was Earl, holding the scaled-down .38 I'd made him give up earlier. He glared at me with adolescent hatred.

"That's him, Marshal!" cried the clerk, pointing a nail-bitten finger at me from behind one of the deputies.

Earl was quaking worse than the last time. "Didn't I say he

was a bad one, Oren? Look at them scratches on his face. You remember the last time we brung one in like that? The judge hung him once for rape and once for murder."

Yardlinger's muddy eyes regarded me, lingering on the scratches, my disheveled clothes, the dust on my knees. Then he looked at the woman.

"What about it, Miss Bower? You want to prefer charges?"

"The lady tried to put a hole in me," I said. "Ask the clerk. He heard the shot."

"That's true," he acknowledged uncertainly.

"Trying to defend herself!" Earl was wound tight.

Yardlinger kept his eyes and his Navy Colt on me. "Miss Bower?"

I looked at Colleen Bower and read nothing in her expression. Tension grew in the silence.

"Randy, take his gun." The former marshal's voice was taut.

One of the armed men stepped forward. Tall and rawboned in a hide jacket, he had wind-burned features and eyes that were bright points of light set in sharp creases, like nailheads driven deep into old wood. His weapon was a double-barreled shotgun cut down to pistol size.

They had me six ways to Wednesday, but I wasn't going to give up my gun in the face of twelve feet of hemp and a short drop to hell. I grasped the butt, ready to pull.

"Wait, Oren," said the woman.

CHAPTER 5

"If you have something to say, you'd better say it damn quick, begging your pardon, ma'am," Yardlinger advised her.

He was standing where he had been when the door opened, sideways astraddle the threshold with his right arm extended and the Navy aimed at my head. Behind him and to his right stood the fourth armed man, a slack-skinned gaffer with gray stubble on his chin, bloodhound eyes, and a Colt Peacemaker nearly as long as a carbine held at chest level in both hands.

"I did take a shot at him," said the woman. "He knocked me down in self-defense."

The deposed marshal took his eyes from me for the first time in a while and it felt as if an anvil had been lifted from my neck. He studied her.

"No offense, but you don't appear to be someone a man would need much defending from."

She fetched her handbag and took out the .32, holding it by its butt between thumb and forefinger, the way my mother used to remove a dead rat from a trap by its tail. She hadn't held it like that twenty minutes earlier.

"Don't you men have a saying about these things being the great equalizers?"

"They say that about the Colt. Different gun. But you made your point." He held his stance. "If it's not too much trouble, maybe you'd care to explain why you shot at a federal officer."

"I caught him searching Bram's room and thought he was a

burglar. I'm afraid I panicked. I was about to shoot again and would have if he hadn't hit me."

The lawman played statue a moment longer, eyes dancing from the woman to me and back again. Then he crooked his arm and let down the hammer on the Colt. "Something about it stinks," he said. "But I'm just the joker in this hand."

"Why don't we haul him in anyhow?" Earl hadn't lowered his weapon. "Could be he's wanted somewhere."

Yardlinger holstered his gun. "Earl, if we locked up everyone in this town who could be wanted somewhere, we wouldn't have cell space for those that are. Put up that toy pistol before you put a hole in United States property. Randy? Major?"

The rawboned deputy lowered the shotgun, followed by the old man, who replaced the Peacemaker's hammer and thrust the gun into his belt. Earl was last to comply. I kept my hand on the Army Colt until Colleen Bower had returned the little Smith to her bag and drawn the string. A disappointed sigh swept through the crowd in the hallway. Yardlinger ordered them to disperse. They obeyed reluctantly and he stepped the rest of the way inside and kicked the door shut.

"Anything else?" he asked the woman.

She shook her head. "Marshal Murdock was about to return some property to me when you came in. I'll just take it and be on my way." She held out her hand for the jewelry case.

"If that's a box full of pretties, we'll hold onto it for now," said Yardlinger.

"You knew about them?" She took an involuntary step backward.

"I found them in that chest of drawers when I came to pick up Bram's clothes for Mrs. Arno. Murdock?"

I gave him the box. "If there's a safe in the office, lock them up. We'll hold them for ten days. If no one claims them in that time we'll return them to the lady."

"Who the hell are you to give orders?" demanded Earl.

I stepped to the door and opened it. "Miss Bower?"

She tilted her chin haughtily, picked up her skirts, and swept out into the now-deserted hallway. Men keep making and buying better firearms, but women have all the weapons. When she was clear of the threshold I closed the door and in the same movement swung around and belted Earl on the chin with the fist I'd used to silence the woman earlier.

He was husky so I put everything I had into it. It wasn't enough. He stumbled backward, slamming into the dressing table and knocking the last of the glass out of the devastated mirror. Then he shook his head and came at me headfirst. He tripped over Yardlinger's outthrust leg and pitched forward his full length to the floor at my feet. The room shook.

"What the hell did you do that for?" Cross barked.

"For this." The former marshal pushed a telegraph form under the weathered deputy's nose. "Blackthorne's confirmation," he said to me. "I was reading it when the clerk came to complain that some rough-looking road agent posing as a deputy marshal was tearing his hotel apart." To Cross, "Murdock's the law in this town until someone in authority says different."

"Not my law he ain't." He started to take off his badge.

"Leave it alone," I said.

He paused, staring down the muzzle of my hip gun.

Earl had started to push himself to his feet. He held his crouch, glaring up at me from under pale brows.

I said, "I've been appointed to keep the peace in Breen, and until I'm off the hook that's what I aim to do. That means I'll need every man in this room. I may hang for it later, but I'll blast a hole a yard wide in whoever reaches for that doorknob."

"He's bluffing," said Earl.

"Raise or call," I countered.

There was a short silence.

"Hell," said a voice, "that's too rich for my blood. I'm in."

I'd almost forgotten the old man, seated now on the edge of the stepping stool next to the bed. His rheumy eyes glistened under his floppy hat as he placed a fresh cut of chewing tobacco skewered on the end of a wicked knife into his mouth. He spoke with a high Ozark twang dragged over Mississippi gravel.

"I like you, mister. You remind me of this here Yankee lieutenant a bunch of us boys cornered in a pigsty by Ox Ford. Sergeant Maddox shot him in the hand when he went for his side arm. He grabbed for it with his other hand and Maddox smashed that one too. Then he threw out his stumps and charged. The Yank warn't three feet off when ole Mad opened a hole in his chest you could drive a four-horse team through. He went down, but you know what? He crawled the rest of the way and bit ole Mad on the leg!"

His cackling turned to a hideous, racking cough and he bubbled off into silent convulsions that ended only when he stuffed a pink-mottled handkerchief into his mouth. He was a saintly old fellow.

"What about it, Randy?" Yardlinger asked the man with the shotgun. "I can handle Murdock's threats. In or out?"

Cross chewed on his ragged moustache. His bullet-like eyes surveyed me without affection. "I don't know," he said. "I ain't ever run from a fight yet, but I can't watch my front and my back at the same time. How do we know he's what he says he is?"

I laughed harshly. "I can't blame you for being suspicious. I bet they're beating down your door to be made lawmen in this town."

He ruminated on that for a moment. "I still don't know. How about you, Oren?"

"I never had any choice in it, you know that."

"Well, if it's good enough for you." I wouldn't have bet a Confederate dollar on the conviction in Cross's voice.

"It ain't good enough for me."

36

I looked down at Earl, who hadn't moved from his starting position on the floor. "Who said I wanted you? Hit the street and leave the star here."

"He's a good man," Yardlinger cautioned.

"He whines too much and he hides his gun. People who don't want you to know they're armed are looking for a chance to squirt one at your back. Besides, I think he's our spy."

"What makes you think so?"

"I don't like him."

The young deputy rose. Upright, he turned the tables and looked down at me as if from a great height. I had known a scalp hunter in the Bitterroots who could have palmed his head in one hand, but in that room he was formidable enough. I wasn't sure I could knock him down a second time even with a bullet.

"I'm as good a man as anyone here." He'd bitten through his lip when struck and the swelling slurred his speech. "Better than some."

"What's this about a spy?" pressed Cross.

Yardlinger filled him in. The old man guffawed.

"Hell, if I knowed someone'd pay for it I'd tell a story or two myself."

"If Earl wants in, I'll vouch for him," said the former marshal.

I stifled a yawn—from fatigue, not insolence. "Who'll vouch for you?"

"Son of a bitch," Cross muttered.

Yardlinger was unmoved. "You've probably been too busy playing the put-upon outsider to notice, but the likelihood of your being elected to Congress in this city hasn't improved since you came. Without me, you don't have deputies, and without deputies—"

"I'm sold. Introduce me."

"You they know." He nodded at each in turn. "That's

37

Randy Cross with the scattergun. He's good with it. Couple of years ago he used one like it to blow the lock off a Wells, Fargo strongbox headed for Deadwood. Pinkertons tracked him down in Canada and he got twenty to life, but he was released for helping put down a riot in territorial prison. He put in time as a railroad detective with James Hill before Bram swore him in here. Earl Trotter's a Breen native and a hell of a fine pistol shot.

"And then there's Leroy Cooperstown Brody."

"*Major* Leroy Cooperstown Brody." The old man squirted a yellow-brown stream at a brass cuspidor six feet away. He hit it square.

"Major Brody commanded a cavalry unit in Virginia during the late hostilities, though I imagine he'd have a hard time recognizing the country in broad daylight."

"Night riders," I said.

Brody made a soggy snapping sound with the plug in his mouth. "The First Virginia Volunteers. Our flag was bonny blue, not black."

"I'm sure that was a source of comfort to the people you murdered," Yardlinger replied. "Anyway, when there's shooting to be done the Major doesn't back off, which is why Bram made him jailer. He doesn't have a badge because I don't want him to go around thinking he's a deputy. That's what you have to work with."

"I've worked with worse."

Yardlinger looked at Earl. "What about it? You've had plenty of time to make up your mind."

The hulking deputy squeezed his torn lower lip between two fingers. "I get to walk out when I don't like it, right?"

"Wrong," I said. "In now, in to the end."

"I got to take orders from him?" Looking at Yardlinger, he jerked his chin at me.

"There's room for only one marshal in any outfit," nodded the other.

"Come on, Earl-boy," twanged the Major. "What you going to do, you don't throw in with us? Go back home and haul plow for your old man?"

"*No!*" The violence of the retort made even the old reprobate jump. "Not for him. I reckon I'm in."

Brody chuckled nastily and took another pass at the cuspidor. This time he barely hit the rim.

"What now?" Yardlinger was watching me.

I considered. "When do you expect the hands from the Six Bar Six?"

"Sundown."

"Unless cowhands have changed, the trouble will start about two minutes after the first one has his belly full of whiskey."

"They haven't changed."

"I counted fourteen saloons. Any more?" He shook his head. I glanced out the window, at the sun straddling the false front of the livery across the street. "We'd best get started. Any temperance folks in town?"

"A few," replied Yardlinger, bewildered.

"Place like this, I don't imagine they have much to sing about."

"Of course not. But what the hell has that—"

"Well, they'll be singing tonight." I began rummaging through drawers. "Help me find the key to that gun rack."

CHAPTER 6

Closing saloons is a shotgun job. At the jail, I used the late lawman's key to unlock the chain securing the long guns, handed an American Arms 12-gauge to Yardlinger and divided a pair of cut-down 10-gauge Remingtons between Earl and the Major. Randy Cross seemed content with his cut-down 12. For myself I selected a Winchester .44 carbine, as no one had yet balanced a scattergun to my satisfaction. Finally I pocketed a handful of cartridges from one of several boxes in the drawer under the rack.

"Take what you need," I said, fitting the padlock back on the chain. "If we're lucky we won't use what's in the chambers, but there's one thickheaded drunk in every saloon."

Yardlinger filled the side pocket of his frock coat with shells for his 12-gauge. "I don't much like this plan. Why don't we just set up a barricade at the end of the street and disarm the hands as they come in?"

"I heard of a Ranger who tried that down in Amarillo," I said. "They never did find enough of him to bury. A cowboy will kill to keep his gun, but not to drink."

"I've seen men kill for less."

"On the range. Not in a town full of witnesses, unless they've already been drinking."

"I guess you know how much faith I put in that," he said dryly.

"That's why the shotguns."

Outside, the sun was draining into the horizon in a wallow

41

of orange and purple. A stiff breeze stirred the dust in the street and laid its cold hand against our faces. On the boardwalk in front of the jail I gestured with the Winchester. "Earl and Randy, take the east side. Start at the other end and work your way back up here. We'll come the same way along the west walk. Don't be afraid to make noise if anyone gives you trouble. One more thing."

The group had started to break up. Everyone looked at me.

"If anyone comes back with liquor on his breath I'll have him stuffed and stood up in the middle of town as a monument to the evils of drink."

Cross and Earl left with a dual snort. I'd impressed the daylights out of them.

Our first stop was the Pick Handle, a shack with canvas tacked over the spaces where boards were missing and one opaque window a foot square. A coal-oil lantern swung from a nail in a rafter, oozing greasy light over a plank laid across two beer kegs that served as the bar. Two men were leaning on it and a short man with a barrel body and a matted tangle of black beard was pouring red whiskey into a glass on the other side. He stopped when he saw our guns.

"Evening, Oren, Major," he said cautiously. "What'll you have?"

I said, "Nothing tonight. These fellows paid for their drinks?" I jerked my head toward the pair watching us from the bar.

The bartender considered the question, then shook his head. His eyes wandered left and down to where a sawed-off shotgun lay across a packing crate.

I tossed a coin onto the plank. It bounced and would have rolled off the edge if he hadn't slapped a meaty hand down on top of it. "They're on me," I announced. "Drain your glasses, gents. It's closing time."

"What the hell!" The bartender grabbed for the shotgun. I

cracked the barrel of the Winchester across the back of his wrist. Howling, he yanked it back.

"Don't," snapped Yardlinger, covering the two customers, one of whom had grasped the handle of a revolver in his belt.

"It's just for tonight," I told the bartender, who was busy testing his injured wrist for breaks. "You don't want to lose the use of that arm over a few dollars." To Yardlinger, indicating the customers: "Either of these Terwilliger's?"

"No."

I held out my hand to the one with the gun. At length he drew it gingerly and placed it in my palm. It was a prewar piece, much in need of cleaning. I stuck it in my belt. "You're lucky you didn't get a chance to pull the trigger and blow your hand off. You can pick it up at the jail later. Get going, both of you." They slunk out. I returned my attention to the man behind the bar. "Lock up."

"How?" He was still rubbing the wrist. "Got no key. The place ain't been closed since it was built."

"Got a hammer and nails and a board?"

He said he did. Yardlinger went with him into the back room and they came out a moment later, the bartender carrying a hammer and a small sack in one hand and a weathered plank four feet long under his other arm. As we accompanied him to the front door his eyes sought Major Brody's.

"Who is this guy?" He gestured at me with the board.

The old man shrugged a thin shoulder. "Anyhow, what's it matter? He's got a weapon and you ain't."

Yardlinger leaned his shotgun beyond the bartender's reach outside and helped him nail the board across the entrance. "That won't keep nobody out," predicted the bartender.

"It won't have to," I said. "Tomorrow you can yank it down and throw it away." We watched while he retreated down the street toward home, carrying his tools. Then we moved on.

We encountered little resistance at the Sunset and French Sam's, establishments similar to the Pick Handle and just about as deserted. The sight of the Major's ravaged face above the 10-gauge, his tobacco plug bulging one cheek, calmed a sodden range cook who had staggered out of his seat to challenge our authority at Sam's. In each location the occupants were driven out and the front door locked from the outside. At the Glory we paused for a consultation before entering.

It was a big building with leaded-glass windows and mineral-oil lamps inside spilling rich yellow light out onto the boardwalk, a far cry from the stark simplicity of the places we'd visited previously. Yardlinger came back from peering over the batwing doors, shaking his head.

"There are six Terwilliger men in there that I can see. And one of the customers we ran out of French Sam's, drinking at the bar. Maybe a dozen others scattered around the room. They'll be ready for us."

"Is there a back way?" I asked.

"Side door off the alley."

As quietly as possible I racked a fresh shell into the Winchester's chamber, ejecting the one that was in there, picked it up and poked it into the magazine. I did it partly out of nervous habit and partly because I never trust a cartridge that hasn't moved in a while. "Who goes in through the front?"

"The Major," said Yardlinger, without hesitation. "No one takes him seriously."

"Should we?" I looked at the old man.

He grinned, showing a black crescent where his teeth should have been. Either molars were all he had left or he gummed his chew. "I ain't used up yet."

I nodded. "Start counting. Give us twenty to reach the side door. No one leaves till I'm finished talking, no one flashes iron. But try not to blow holes in too many of Breen's upstanding citizens."

"Hell, that's no restriction. They ain't none."

"Just don't forget this isn't Virginia and it isn't eighteen

44

sixty-three," I cautioned. "I'm just getting used to having you around and I wouldn't want to see you stretching a rope."

I reminded him to count to twenty and struck off down the narrow alley with the other deputy. The sun was almost below the horizon, and except for a thin yellow L outlining the door we were surrounded by darkness. We hesitated before going in.

"Where are the cowhands?" My breath curled out in wisps of vapor.

"Two at the bar when I looked," said Yardlinger. "Three more sharing a table west of the front door opposite. Last one playing poker next to the bar with three other customers, one of them the guy we chased out of Sam's. You want to watch the Terwilliger man playing cards. Name's Pardee. It was his brother the vigilantes almost lynched. He'll be smoking a cigar. Never leaves his mouth."

"I'll take the bar side. You cover the three at the table. And watch out for everyone else. The man who gets the last shot is always the last one you suspect. Let's go."

I pushed the door open noiselessly and we crossed through a dim storeroom stacked with kegs and barrels and reeking of old beer and new vomit, the one thing all saloons have in common, to an open door through which bar sounds were leaking. As we approached, the buzz of voices in the outer room died. Major Brody had entered.

All eyes were on him as we stepped inside. A frumpy figure in a stained coat and trousers that bagged at the knees, he was standing at the end of an aisle that ran between the tables and a bar of glossy dark wood trimmed with brass. The huge twin barrels of his truncated Remington were trained on the room at large. His sagging hat brim masked his eyes and his tobacco cud raised a hard knot beneath his right ear.

"Who the hell are you supposed to be, Major?" The bartender, heavy-muscled in a calico shirt and tight silk vest, kept his hands hidden behind the bar. He had blunt features like an Indian and an upper lip that curled back and flattened under his nose when he smiled, exposing long, slightly discolored teeth. I figured him for an opium smoker and wondered if there were any Chinese in town.

"Who don't matter," explained Brody in a dead voice. "It's what you'll be if you don't get them hands in plain sight, Alf. Which is dead."

"I thought you guerrilla fellows generally went in for back shooting."

"So do lawmen," I said. "When it's convenient."

Alf jerked around, seeing Yardlinger and me for the first time. His left arm moved spasmodically. I shouted at him to hold it and came around the end of the bar, keeping the carbine pointed at his thick hard belly. There was a row of beer pulls behind the bar to his left, including one that didn't match the others. I grasped it and tugged a Schofield revolver out of a greased socket.

"For shame," I said, and backhanded him across his flat face, laying the revolver's long barrel along his right cheekbone. He clapped a hand to the cheek and staggered back against the shelves behind the bar. Bottles clattered. He took his hand away and looked at his fingers. There was no blood, but a reddish welt had risen under his eye.

Major Brody chuckled. Yardlinger stared at me in surprise, then remembered himself and swung his shotgun to take in his side of the room.

While the Major covered the bar side I rested the Winchester in the crook of my arm, unloaded the Schofield, and dropped it and the cartridges into a bucket of dirty mop water at my feet. The splash and clunk was loud in the silence of the room.

"That ain't no way to treat a good gun."

I looked at the speaker, a round-faced man, clean-shaven, with a long cigar screwed into the center of his mouth, calmly dealing cards at a table next to the bar. His fine blond hair was parted just above his left ear and combed across his scalp to make up for what he'd lost on top. In his town suit he looked as much like a cowhand as I looked like Eddie Foy. I recognized one of the three silent men seated with him as a lounger I had driven from French Sam's.

I said, "Who says the Schofield's a good gun?"

"Jesse James, for one."

"That explains how he blew the raid on Northfield. You're Pardee?"

He threw away two cards and slid two more from the deck. "You're Murdock."

"Now that we're on a last-name basis, let's talk. You know some men are on their way here from Dick Mather's spread."

"I heard something on that order. In for two." He tossed a pair of chips into the center of the table.

"Talk is you think it was Mather's boys almost strung up your brother."

"See it and raise you five." The man from Sam's sweetened the pot. The man at his right folded. The fourth man equaled the bet.

"Raise ten." More chips left Pardee's stack.

"Trying to buy the pot," grumbled the fourth player.

"It'll cost him." The man from Sam's saw the raise.

I leaned across the bar and brought the barrel of the Winchester smashing down atop the table. Chips and cards flew.

"Goddamn!" Pardee reached for his hip.

A roar shook the room. The cigar smoker's hand sprang away empty. In the loud silence that followed, everyone in the room gaped at the Major, standing in a cloud of swirling blue smoke, his shotgun pointed at the ceiling and a litter of plaster around his feet. He chewed casually.

"Hey!" The bartender was first to shake off the spell. "Who's going to pay for that?"

Brody drew his lips tight against his gums and shot a stream at the nearest cuspidor. "I reckon Pardee's the man you should talk to about that. It was him startled me into yanking this here trigger, going to scratch that there itch on his hip so sudden."

"The idea was to get your attention," I told Pardee. "Why do you think Six Bar Six riders are responsible for what happened to your brother?"

The cowhand took the cigar from his mouth, spat out bits of tobacco, and crushed it out in a crystal ashtray full of chewed brown butts on the table. In the excitement he had bitten through it. He lit another. Puffing it into life: "Six Bar Six, Périgueux, what difference does it make? They was trying to scare me into quitting as foreman. They know I don't rabbit when it's just my hide, so they tried to get at me through Dale. If I leave, Terwilliger goes under. He can't get no one else to ramrod with things like they are."

"So what's going to happen tonight?"

"I reckon that's between me and that consumptive bastard."

"I reckon not. The law's here now. We'll take care of Mather, if Mather's behind the raids."

"How?" He snapped the still-burning match into the mounded tray. "You going to throw the old bushwhacker in front of Dick's horse and trip it up?"

Mild laughter bubbled around the room. The Major went on chewing as if he hadn't heard. His shoulders and the crown of his hat were white from the plaster dust that was still dribbling from the gaping hole in the ceiling.

"Whose idea was it to bring in Chris Shedwell?" I asked Pardee. "Yours or Terwilliger's?"

He restacked his chips. "Wouldn't make much sense, would it? Us hiring him and then me coming here to square things myself."

He had a point.

"You're a gambling man," I said. "I'll make you a bet." Tucking the Winchester under my arm, I came around the bar and gathered up the scattered cards with my free hand.

When the deck was intact I shuffled and dealt us each five. Then I peeled a five-dollar bill off the roll in my pocket and laid it on the table. "If I don't arrest the men who hoorawed your brother in a week, you can even things up your own way, short of killing."

Pardee pursed his lips around the cigar, drumming his fingers on the cards I'd dealt him face down. At length he picked up a chip and somersaulted it expertly across his knuckles and back, turning it over in the cracks between.

"And if you arrest them?"

"Call off the feud. Consider yourself square with Mather and Périgueux. For my part, I'll see that the night riders stand trial for abduction and malicious mischief. But I'll do it my way, which includes shutting down this saloon tonight."

He frowned at the chip as he manipulated it faster and faster, back and forth across his hand. Then he snapped it off his thumb. It rolled over in the air several times and landed flat atop my five dollars. "Pick up your cards."

I did, arranging them and placing them face up on the table. I had a pair of jacks. He glanced at them, nodded, and turned his over. Three sixes and two kings stared up at me impassively.

"Full house," he announced. "Sure hope you're not on a sour streak, Marshal."

CHAPTER 7

The Terwilliger crew left, some reluctantly but not inclined to argue with their foreman, and soon we heard their hoofbeats receding in the direction of the ranch. With them gone, the bartender at the Glory saw little point in stopping us from closing the place even if he had wanted to, which evidently he didn't any more. He helped us roust out the more stubborn customers, turned out the lamps, and locked up, grasping his dripping revolver uselessly in one hand. I sent him off with a reminder to send the bill for the damaged ceiling to the marshal's office and a warning not to jack up the amount.

We found the last two saloons on our side of the street dark, the doors already locked. Our fame was spreading. As we turned away from the final stop, Yardlinger said, "Why bother anyway? With Pardee and his boys out of town we've got nothing to worry about. Why not let Mather's hands drink up and go?"

"Two reasons. First, if we let them get a snootful in the mood they'll be in, they might decide to go hunting for Terwilliger men or take out their frustration on some other target." I paused while he set fire to a cheroot.

"Second?" He squirted smoke through his nostrils and watched the flame on his match creep close to his fingers. It was dark out, the only illumination a ghostly glow from the fogged windows of the hotels and late-closing shops.

"Second, a lawman has to finish what he starts, or folks get to thinking he's soft. If he keeps changing his mind, they'll wonder if anything he says is worth much."

"That why you pistol-whipped Alf back at the Glory?"

I sighed. "I was wondering when you'd get around to that."

"You didn't have to hit him. You had his gun."

"I didn't do it for him. I did it for the others in the room who were watching. The Major understands. He fired his scattergun through the roof for the same reason."

The old guerrilla shifted his plug from one cheek to the other. "You said not to be afeared of making noise."

"So the bartender puts steak on his eye and the ceiling gets a patch," I said. "Beats the cost of burial."

"I don't think that's the reason you hit him," insisted the former marshal. "I think it was because you liked it."

For a moment we stood watching each other in the gloom. Smoke drifted straight up from the glowing end of his cheroot in the motionless air before it was caught and blown ragged by the wind above brim level. Then there was a noise in the street and all three of us spun in that direction, long guns ready. Randy Cross and Earl Trotter mounted the boardwalk.

"Next time announce yourself," I snarled in my relief. "Another second and you'd have been breathing out your belly."

Cross ignored the comment. "Well, they're shut down on our side. If there's a drop of alcohol to be got in town, it's horse liniment."

"Any trouble?"

"Couple of prospectors tried to jump Randy in the House of Mirrors," said Earl. "I asked them not to."

The other deputy snorted. "He kicked one in the belly and clubbed the other across the knees with his shotgun. You should of heard him howl. First one's still heaving, I reckon."

"That's the way I used to make Pa's horses behave," shrugged the younger man.

I turned to Yardlinger. "How many cathouses in town?"

"Just one, Martha's, over on Arapaho. But she serves claret.

A man'd be all night getting drunk enough to start anything."

"Just so we know where they'll be if they decide to stick."

"That's them now," said Cross.

Rumbling hoofbeats swelled as a dozen riders swung into the north end of the street, trailing a fog of horses' breath. I pointed at the open doors of the livery stable, each of which sported a burning lantern hanging on a nail. "Confiscate those and bring them along."

Earl obeyed, ignoring the protests of the old Negro in charge, and hurried to catch up with us. As we approached the riders, the thunder of hoofs faltered and died. The darkness on the street had alerted the newcomers. Steel slid from leather, hammers rolled back with a racheting sound.

When the lanterns arrived I took one and held it up as I walked across in front of the line of horsemen.

Dick Mather regarded me in hostile silence, a sick man slumped in a linen duster and gripping the pommel of his saddle in both hands as if to keep from toppling off. The man to his immediate right had a broken nose and one thick black eyebrow that went straight across both eyes, giving him a primitive look that was completed by his close-cropped black beard. The gun in his left hand was a Smith & Wesson American .44. The other riders were ten years younger, but their faces were as hard as the weapons they brandished.

I finished my inspection and returned to Yardlinger's side. The five of us were strung out across the street, forming a human barricade with guns in hand.

"That's Abel Turk next to Mather, the bearded one," the chief deputy informed me. "Foreman at the Six Bar Six. He hasn't seen many backs hereabouts since his reputation got around."

"What's going on, Murdock?" demanded the rancher in his phlegmy baritone. "Whole town in mourning for Marshal Arno?"

"Not until his replacement dried up the watering holes," I

replied. "You're welcome to stay as long as you like, boys, but there'll be no drinking tonight."

"What gives you that right?" The man Yardlinger had identified as Abel Turk spoke quietly, with no threat in his deep voice. Never trust a man who's slow to anger. I looked him over again, then returned to Mather.

"Don't you tell your hands anything?"

"He told me some hot iron who calls himself Murdock is playing lawman," Turk said. "That still don't give you leave to refuse a thirsty cowman a drink."

"Maybe it doesn't. But this does." I patted the carbine.

"We aren't breaking any laws," huffed Mather.

"You're flashing a lot of steel for law-abiding citizens."

He let that go. "You running us out of town?"

"Not at all. Like you said, you haven't broken any laws. But if you try to get into one of the saloons, I'll arrest you all for breaking and entering. I understand there's an open door on Arapaho Street."

"No thanks." The rancher gathered his reins. His shaggy gray tossed its head and whinnied softly, clouds of steam billowing from its nostrils. "I never did take to keeping all my chickens in one henhouse when there's a skunk loose."

I grinned. "There's an insult in there somewhere, but you're forgiven. Any word from Helena?"

"I sent your boss a wire asking him to relieve you as city marshal. I haven't heard anything yet. He must keep banker's hours. What are you smirking about?"

"Life in general," I replied. Blackthorne had been in his office at least once since we'd parted, to confirm Yardlinger's query about my appointment. Ignoring Mather's request meant he wanted me to stay on as marshal. I didn't know why. His contrariness had been known to cause strokes among his superiors in Washington City.

The rancher's fever-sunken eyes darted to Yardlinger. "You in on this?"

54

"I do what I'm told." The former marshal's tone was non-committal.

"What about the rest of you?"

Cross and Earl kept silent, letting their shotguns say it all. Major Brody spat tobacco at the gray's left forefoot, missing the hoof by less than an inch. The animal shied and blew out its nostrils.

Mather's breath whistled in his throat. Without a word he backed his horse out of line, wheeled, and spurred north. It took his men a moment to grasp that he was leaving, and then Turk replaced the hammer on the big American and rammed it into its holster. I caught the glitter of his eyes as he raked them over me, burning my face and figure into his memory. Then they were all gone in a cloud of dust.

"Twenty dollars says we'll see them again," I said, lowering the Winchester.

Yardlinger laid both his hammers carefully against the caps in the 12-gauge. "No bet."

"I'm thirsty," announced the Major.

I wasn't, but I needed a drink. "Is there a bottle in the office?"

"If you don't mind a dead man's liquor," the chief deputy nodded. "It belonged to Marshal Arno."

No one objected. Once the lamp was lit in the office, I replaced four of the long guns in the rack along with the extra ammunition while Yardlinger excavated the bottle and Major Brody mopped out the bore of his Remington with oil and a rod. Earl, who had lagged behind to return the borrowed lanterns to the livery, entered just as the cork was pulled.

"That isn't store whiskey," I commented, looking at the crystal-clear liquid in the bottle.

"That's pure-oldie Masie-Dixie sippin' shine," whistled the Major. "Hunnert and ten proof."

"Longer it sits the stronger it gets," Yardlinger warned. "Bram wasn't much of a drinking man. He took it for evi-

55

dence from a runner he arrested for introducing to the Cheyennes more than a year ago. I guess the marshal forgot he had it. The fellow hanged himself in his cell."

I said, "Don't talk, pour."

"Only one glass." He held up an amber-tinted container not much bigger than a thimble.

"Who needs it?" The Major seized the bottle.

So we sat around in chairs and on the oak railing, passing the vessel back and forth like kids in a barn, while Major Brody regaled us with progressively gorier war stories. The liquor was harsh and tasted of cork. After Earl's first pull and a fit of prolonged coughing, he left, and then the drinking got serious.

Somewhere a clock struck nine and Cross weaved out, mumbling something about dinner, a wife, and the imminence of violent death. Half an hour later the Major's monologue dropped to a growl and then silence. When he failed to respond the next time the bottle came around I made an effort to get out of my chair, then gave up and leaned forward, bracing my right arm with my left hand to tug open his eyelids.

"Well, he isn't dead."

"How can you tell?" said Yardlinger, and started giggling. Someone else was laughing, high and quick like an idiot. I wondered who it was.

"I was just thinking—" He choked and went back to giggling.

I felt the laughter bubbling back up and tried to put it down with another swallow. Some of the whiskey got in my mouth. "What?"

"I was just thinking," he said again, and gasped for air.

"Thinking what?"

"That we had about seven chances of getting killed tonight, and that if we did the city council would have been faced with the problem of appointing their third marshal in two days."

I was in the middle of another pull. I choked and he leaned across the desk to slap me mightily on the back, nearly falling over when he missed. I laughed then, so clearly and loudly I can hear it to this day. It was the funniest thing anyone had ever said. He laughed too. It went on like that for the better part of a minute, and when it died we looked at each other and started in again. Finally we were played out. I pushed the bottle across to him. There was a quarter inch left in the bottom.

"Who's Colleen Bower?"

"Who?" He was leaning as far back in the swivel chair as he could without going over, his head resting on the back and his eyes closed. His profile was limned in pale yellow from the low-burning lamp.

I repeated the name and tried to trace the outline of a female figure in the air with my hands. The result was closer to a bull fiddle, but I got my meaning across.

"No one knows for sure." The stove had gone out and his breath curled when he spoke. "She claims to have been a schoolteacher in Arkansas, but I don't credit it. For a while she called herself Poker Annie and dealt faro in and around the Nations. We got a reader on her a year ago, which was about the time she came to Breen. Couple of half-breeds got themselves shot up over her in Yankton. She cleared out right after and the U.S. marshal wanted to know what happened to a thousand dollars in gold one of the breeds lifted from the express office in Bismarck. Bram arrested her at the Glory where she was dealing and wired Yankton to come get her. Turned out they didn't want her any more. They'd found the gold in the Bismarck express clerk's closet."

"Arresting someone's a strange way to begin a courtship. You going to finish what's in that bottle or not?"

He opened his eyes and lifted it from the desk, missing the

first time he reached for it. The contents drained, he replaced it carefully, using both hands. It fell over, rolled to the edge, and quivered there like a baby bird getting ready for its first flight.

"I think the rest of it was her idea," he said, watching the bottle. "Gamblers who expect to die in bed have two rules: don't get caught cheating and try to stay on the sunny side of the local law. That last part's easy when you wear petticoats."

"Where's she staying?" I could barely hear myself. I was warm from the alcohol and pleasantly drowsy.

"She's got a room at Martha's. What makes you so interested?"

"She's a double portion of woman."

He tried to focus on me, then gave up and returned his attention to the teetering vessel. "I might believe that's your reason if I didn't know you had black powder for blood."

"You wrong me cruelly."

"Sabers at dawn," he suggested, and flicked a finger at the bottle. It thudded to the floor without breaking and rolled to a rest against a leg of my chair. Then he got up, clawing at the edge of the desk for support.

Stumbling over to where the Major slumped snoring in a broken chair with his toothless mouth wide open, Yardlinger bumped into furniture a couple of times and placed a finger to his lips, shushing himself. Carefully he plucked the shotgun from the old man's grasp and returned it to the rack. When the chain was secure he curled up in the middle of a colorful Indian rug on the floor behind the desk and went to sleep with his hands under his head. I remember resenting him for taking the best spot in the room, after which I don't remember much of anything.

I felt fine the next morning until I opened my eyes.

CHAPTER 8

Light showed pink through my eyelids. When I finally got them unstuck, slow pain opened in my skull like a dirty blossom and found the spot where the Bower woman had tried to split it open with her gun. I closed my eyes and waited for merciful sleep to overtake me again. When it didn't I opened them more carefully, shielding them with a hand from daylight as I levered myself out of the chair. Every muscle in my body had something to say about it.

Major Brody remained as we had left him, dragging air through a mouth gaped wide enough to tempt bats. I glanced toward the rug but Yardlinger was gone. At that moment he came in through the opening in the partition holding a wet washrag on the back of his neck. His face was puffy and unshaven.

When he saw me he snarled something about a basin in back. I thumped off in that direction, wondering if I looked as bad as he did. The wavy mirror over the basin said I looked worse.

He had thrown out his wash water, but the pitcher under the stand was half full. I poured some of its contents into the bowl and stuck my head in as far as it would go. It wasn't far enough. I toweled off and returned to the office. The Major's chair was empty.

"Went home," Yardlinger explained from his seat at the desk. "Chipper as a goddamn squirrel. He said the closest he ever came to dissipation was the time a Kansas jayhawker broke a Springfield rifle stock over his head. I told him that didn't qualify."

I placed my hat gingerly on my head. "Watch the office. If you've got a razor here you might do something to make yourself presentable. You look like a mile and a half of collapsed tunnel."

"You don't look like Edwin Booth in *Hamlet*."

My riding clothes were waiting for me at the Freestone, freshly cleaned and brushed. I put them on after a bath and a careful shave (the scratches from my Breen House adventure had scabbed over nicely) and gave my wrinkled city trappings to the attendant for the same treatment. In the restaurant next door I forced myself to eat a hearty breakfast, ignoring the curious looks of nearby diners as I scribbled with a pencil stub on a linen napkin. Word of last night's adventure had gotten around.

Next I presented myself at the office of the Breen *Democrat* on Mandan Street, where a chest-high counter separated me from a wainscoted chamber in which a man in shirtsleeves rolled up past his elbows and a greasy leather apron was screwing down a huge flatbed press. Nearby, a boy not much older than fourteen selected pieces of lead type from a flat case and slid them into a composing stick in his left hand. Stacks of brown newsprint and bound papers left only narrow aisles to walk through, and black ink was smeared over everything, including the man at the press.

I waited five minutes and then rapped my knuckles on the counter top. The press man glanced up irritably.

"Keep your drawers on. Newspapers don't run themselves."

Some more time passed, and then he climbed down from a step plate built onto the machine, set aside an oilcan he had been using to lubricate the big screw, and crab-walked between dangerously leaning piles of paper to the counter, stopping once to light a charred black pipe taken from his hip pocket. He was small and lean, in his late fifties, and had a shock of unkempt brown hair that looked black because of the ink in it.

"How soon can I have a hundred of these printed up?" I unfolded the napkin I'd borrowed from the restaurant and spread it out on the counter. He took a pair of wire-rimmed spectacles from a shirt pocket and hooked them on one ear at a time to read what I'd written.

"'Reward,'" he read tonelessly. "'One hundred dollars for information leading to the arrest and conviction of one or all of the culprits responsible for illegal harassment of employees at the Terwilliger ranch. See P. Murdock, acting city marshal.'" He peeled aside the spectacles. "You P. Murdock?"

The boy at the typecase turned to stare at me.

I admitted I was Murdock. The man said, "Maybe this will interest you," and left me to skin a broadsheet off the bed of the press. Holding it by the corners he returned to the counter and draped it over the top. "Ink's wet," he warned.

Half of the center two columns was claimed by a line drawing of a jowly old jasper with sad eyes and a great white handlebar moustache, encircled by a black wreath. The caption read:

ABRAHAM SHELLEY ARNO

1828–1879

Friend and Champion

"Folks around here hold the late marshal in high regard, do they?" I asked.

The newspaperman made an impolite noise around the stem of his pipe. "The old bastard. Last week I ran an editorial calling for his dismissal on the grounds of early senility. But that isn't what I wanted you to see. Third column, at the end of all that horse dung about Arno's years of service."

It was headed NEW MARSHAL IMPOSES PROHIBITION:

Page Murdock, Breen City Marshal by no other authority than the whim of United States Judge Harlan A.
Blackthorne, spent his first hours in office yesterday evening closing down every drinking establishment on Pawnee Street. "Strong drink is at the bottom of man's baser
passions," sources close to the peace officer have quoted
him as saying. "Remove it, and you remove the need for
law enforcement itself." Owners and patrons of the establishments visited by Murdock and his deputies found
their protestations met with guns.

Our question is this: Does Marshal Murdock really
yearn so strongly for unemployment, and if he does, is it
not our duty as citizens to do everything in our power to
fulfill that yearning?

I met the newspaperman's impassive gaze. "Who are the
'sources close to the peace officer,' or did you make them up?"

"If you want to refute the story, write us a letter to the editor. I acknowledge no arguments beyond the columns of the
Democrat."

"If you knew what my head feels like this morning, you
wouldn't accuse me of teetotaling."

"I thought your eyes looked a little bloodshot."

I tapped the napkin with my scrawl on it. "Are you going
to print my handbills or do I have to do them myself in long-
hand?"

"Five dollars."

"Bill me at the office."

"In advance." He held out an inkstained palm.

I gave it to him. "You know what they call a man who
doesn't trust anyone."

"A newspaperman."

He said the handbills would be ready that afternoon and

gave me a receipt, after which I dropped by the gunsmith's to learn that the Swede was fitting the Deane-Adams' new grip. I said I'd check back later. Returning to the office, I found Yardlinger at the desk adding new wanted posters to a dog-eared folder nearly full of them. He still looked like someone who had had too much to drink the night before, but at least he had shaved.

"Telegram came for you." He indicated an envelope on the corner of the desk.

I tore it open. It was signed by Blackthorne.

SWAMPED WITH PROTESTS STOP   CITIZENRY CALL-ING YOU CONDEMNED TEMPERANCE WOMAN STOP WHAT THE DEUCE HAPPENING

"Condemned" was Western Union's prim substitute for "damned." I wondered about "deuce" for a moment, decided it wasn't important anyway, and disposed of the litter in the stove. "Anything else?"

He smirked. "Poker Annie didn't come around asking for you, if that's what you mean."

I didn't acknowledge. I had hoped he'd forget that part of last night's alcoholic conversation. "I'll spell you at noon." I turned back toward the door.

"Where are you going now?"

"Martha's."

He raised his eyebrows. "In broad daylight?"

"Business," I said.

"Yours or hers?"

I told him to go to hell and left.

The den of ill fame was a pleasant-looking whitewashed frame building two stories high, set back from the street with a freshly winnowed lawn between it and the boardwalk. Tu-lips were budding in boxes attached to the ground-floor windows, promising better things later in the season. As I turned into the short walk I was passed by a hatchet-faced woman in a dull charcoal dress who picked up her skirts and her pace with a loud "Hmph!"

The brass door knocker made a genteel sound, followed by a short silence and then a slight shifting of floorboards as footsteps approached. Colleen Bower opened the door.

She was wearing chocolate brown today, relieved only by a dash of ivory-colored lace at her neck. Her hair was up and a dust of powder effectively concealed the discoloration on her jaw. She recognized me and tried to take an impression of my face with my side of the door. I leaned my shoulder against it.

"Why so testy? I thought we'd made up."

"That was before I found out I couldn't eat solid food." She spoke through her teeth.

I touched my scratches. "At least you don't have to shave."

"You can live without shaving. Liquid diets are for geraniums."

"Is it any worse than what they serve in jail?"

She glared. The gold flecks in her eyes seemed to spin and give off their own light. "So you checked up on me. Did they tell you about the time I was almost hanged in New Mexico?"

"That story hasn't reached here yet. What did you do?"

"Took cattle in trade. Some of them turned out to be stolen. Now that you know more than you did coming in, I'm sure you'll excuse me. There's a draft." She tried again to push the door shut, but my body was still in the way.

"I'm on official business," I explained. "Is Martha in?"

"I'm in."

The voice was mannish, like its owner. When Colleen turned her head I saw Martha standing before a beaded curtain in a doorway opposite, tall and square-shouldered in a severe black dress closed at the neck with an emerald brooch. She had a firm jaw, and the bones of her face protruded sharply

64

from the frame of her hair, brushed back into a black halo like
Japanese women wore in the indelicate prints butchers sold in
the back room, and pinned in place. She nodded slightly at
Colleen, who opened the door wider and stepped aside. I entered and the door was closed.

"Martha Foster." The older woman gave me her hand. It
was warm but dry and nearly as large as mine. "I'm sorry,
Marshal, but the maid is out and we can't offer you the hospi-
tality we're famous for."

Colleen executed a cold curtsy and rustled out, leaving me
alone in a room full of too much furniture with a woman as
tall as I was. Martha Foster had a faint moustache and one
milky eye from a cataract, but she held her head like a grand
lady. She looked amused.

"I think Colleen likes you."

I laid my hat on a pedestal table covered with a lace shawl.
"Last time she saw me she tried to part my scalp with a bullet. Just now she made a spirited effort to rearrange my features with your front door. I'd hate to have her fall in love
with me."

"That's just her way. But you haven't come to ask me for
her hand."

"Not if her nails go with it," I said. "I suppose you know
about my agreement with Pardee."

"Very little happens in Breen that I don't know about, Marshal. Men tell things to women in my line. Which is why
you're here, I would guess."

"You're a very canny woman, Mrs. Foster."

"Please. Martha," she said, smiling tightly.

CHAPTER 9

She offered me a chintz-covered armchair but I declined, inviting as it looked. My muscles were still complaining from the ride from Helena and last night's excesses, and there was no guarantee I'd be able to get out of it when the time came.

"I'll only be a minute," I explained. "What I'm after is a drunken boast, a chance comment overheard by one of your girls that might lead me to whoever's been terrorizing Terwilliger's waddies. It's a kid thing. Chances are it'll never come to trial, but an honest effort on my part with some kind of result might head off a range war. That kind of thing is bad business for everybody."

"Everybody but us," she corrected. "Range wars bring guns and men to operate them. The only thing I have to worry about in this business is a shortage of men."

"I expect they'll start getting short soon enough. Does that mean you won't help?"

"I can't. There are no secrets here. If anything important had passed about those raids, I'd have heard. I haven't."

I breathed some air. "I was afraid of that. From what I've seen of Périgueux and Mather, they're not the type to hire flapjaws. If they're behind it. What about the Frenchman? Is he a customer?"

She shook her head. The milk-eye refused to glitter like its mate in the sunlight sifting through the door fan. "He has a wife with whom he appears to be content." There was the least suggestion of disrespect in her pronunciation of the word "wife."

"Dick Mather?"

"Mather is married too, and I'm told he's very sick. I doubt that he's thought of a woman in months."

Next time, I told myself, I'd make my wagers with the cards face up. "I suppose all the cowhands come here."

"Most of them."

"I'd appreciate it if you'd ask the girls to keep their ears open. If they hear anything, I'd take it as a personal favor if you'd pass it along."

She smiled, keeping her lips pressed tight. I'd noticed that when she spoke she held her hand in front of her mouth. Bad teeth were one of the lesser evils of her profession. "Don't misunderstand me, Marshal. I have nothing against casting my bread upon the waters, as long as I can expect something more than soggy crusts in return. To be coarse, what's in it for me?"

"Breen must have a fire ordinance," I said, "and if it doesn't, it will. I doubt that all this furniture cluttering the escape route would fit its guidelines. It might become my duty to close you down until the proper adjustments were made. The decision to allow you to reopen would also be mine, based on a thorough inspection."

"Your predecessor proposed something of the sort." She was still smiling. "It had to do with a fee for protection from damage and robbery. He didn't get it. We entertain some influential people."

"I don't answer to local authority."

"So I heard. Unlike the situation with the saloons, however, there are men willing to defend our right to dispense our services, with guns. It could be very untidy. But there is a way we can agree."

"I'm listening."

Her head was turned slightly to bring her good eye square

on my face. "You may have noticed that this building bunts up against the harness shop next door. The structures share a common wall. I'd like to buy the shop, cut an arch into it, and expand my operation before the railroad comes. But this town has strict deadlining ordinances and the good ladies of Breen have bullied the council into denying me access. If someone were to persuade them to reconsider, I'd be willing to take your request under advisement."

"That's a lot to pay for information that may never come."

"Those are my terms."

I picked up my hat. "You'll be hearing from me."

"Our door is always open, Marshal." She walked me to it.

I went from there to the telegraph office, where I killed an hour drafting a full report of my activities up to that point for the Judge and sent it collect. Then I hastened out before the answer came.

The Swede was perched on a high stool behind the glass counter, eating lunch from a greasy bag when I entered the gunsmith's shop. I could smell his hardboiled egg sandwich from the doorway. He set aside the half he was eating and climbed down chewing to transfer the English revolver from the workbench to the counter. My fingers curled around the walnut grip like a woman embracing her lover after a long separation. It felt good. The sight was true, and when I freed the cylinder it spun without a catch.

"You're a true artist," I said, thrusting the gun under one arm while I dug out a ten, the balance of the price.

"Been told that." The Swede held the bill up to the light and popped it, then folded it in quarters, and poked it into a pocket of his vest. "Compliments don't buy doodly."

I bought a box of .45 cartridges in a brand that fit the Deane-Adams and left him sitting on his stool, picking up where he'd left off on his odorous sandwich. Back at the hotel I dismantled the new gun, laying the parts out carefully on the bedspread, and wiped each part with an oily rag from the kit I carried in a cigar box. I used a clean rag to remove the excess and put the whole thing back together. It hadn't needed cleaning; that was just my way of getting acquainted.

Finally I unbuckled the belt and holster I was wearing and put on the one I'd brought with me from the capital, designed for the gun I'd lost in Dakota. The rig seemed light even after I'd loaded the five-shot. I walked up and down the length of the room to get the feel of it before going back out.

"You're five minutes late," observed Yardlinger, putting away his watch and reaching for his hat. "I hope she was worth it."

It took me a moment to realize he was referring to my stop at Martha's. "Don't be disrespectful. Have Earl spell me at two. I've got an errand to run this afternoon."

"I'll tell him five minutes after."

After he left I wasted some time with my feet on the desk and my hat tilted forward over my eyes the way lawmen did in the *New York Detective Library*, and when I tired of that I went through the drawers, found the yellowback novel Earl had been reading the day before, and began reading. My study was uninterrupted by shooting in the street or window-smashing barroom brawls or runaway horse teams towing the banker's screaming daughter. Next to a cell, the marshal's office in a western town was the dullest place this side of Commodore Vanderbilt's drawing room. It got so I looked forward to the occasional trips from the woodbox to the stove.

Earl came in just as I was finishing the book. I tucked the loose pages into place the way you straighten up a deck of cards, dropped it back into its drawer, and rose, my backside feeling as if it had been slapping a saddle all day.

"How do I get to Périgueux's ranch?" I adjusted my hat.

He checked the stove, decided it didn't need stoking, and pushed the lid shut. "Ride due east from anywhere in the world and you can't miss it. Why?"

"I've got poker fever. Think I'll offer the Marquis a piece of Pardee's action."

"Huh?"

"Mind the store."

I was riding a white-faced roan stallion that year, with one walleye and a disposition like a trodden snake. The old Negro who looked after the livery stable appeared glad to see me and rolled back a checked cotton sleeve to show me two semi-circular bruises on his forearm where he'd been bitten while strapping on the feedbag. I paid him for the horse's care to that point and tipped him handsomely. He couldn't write, so I scribbled the transaction on the back of Blackthorne's last telegram and got his mark.

The roan made a halfhearted attempt to reach back and nip me as I was mounting, but I ignored it and he didn't follow through. He remembered the first time he'd tried that and the taste of blood on his tongue when I kicked him in the teeth. We understood each other.

It was shaping up to be a fine spring day as I cleared the city limits and swung east. The air was crisp—my breath was a quick gray jet that vanished as soon as it left my mouth—but the sun was pasted alone on a construction-paper sky and hills of dead grass described wavy lines of fuzzy yellow crayon between the mountain ranges to east and west. The scenery looked like a child's drawing.

The sun was an hour down when a solitary rider crested a rise a couple of miles ahead, moving fast across country. He dropped out of sight behind the next hill, reappearing closer a few minutes later as he came to the top of that one, then vanishing again. By the time he came over the fourth swell I could see that he had a rifle crossed behind his saddle horn. I loosened the Deane-Adams in its holster and kept riding, cursing myself for leaving behind the Winchester.

He pulled up four hundred yards short and sat waiting. He had a buttermilk horse with a white mane like you see in the

Wild West shows, that lashed its head up and down on a long neck, shaking it with a wobbling motion.

The road swung right past him. When the distance closed to a hundred and fifty yards the rider brought his rifle upright, bracing it on his pelvis. I slowed up after another fifty and stopped. My roan shied toward the road edge and the new grass beginning to poke through the surface. I reined its head back to face the other rider. His horse pawed the ground and looked bored. He didn't.

"This here's Périgueux land," he announced in a high, clear voice that rang like a new penny on a polished counter.

He was even younger than Earl, about eighteen. His yellow hair was long as a girl's and he wore rimless spectacles that flashed white in the sun. His Stetson was the color of dried sweat and dust and his jeans had faded to match the hide of his fleece-lined jacket. The only thing bright about him was a red bandana knotted loosely at his throat. His rifle was one I hadn't seen before, which for me was going some. A single-shot from the look of it, it had a long barrel and a lever shaped like a question mark, and looked about as native as his employer's accent. For all I knew it could fire out both ends and never need cleaning.

"I'm Murdock, here to see Périgueux," I explained. "Likely he's mentioned me."

He chewed on that for a space. He had thick lips that slacked open and a gap between his front teeth. "Let's see something."

Keeping my right hand hidden, I dug the first two fingers of my left into my shirt pocket and flipped the star over his head like a coin. He lost it in the sun for a moment, then spotted it on the way down and snatched at it with his free hand. It sprang out of his reach with a twang that was swallowed by the accompanying report. The echo growled in the distant mountains and died hissing.

His reflexes were fast. He swung the rifle down between the

shot and the echo, but I recocked the Deane-Adams and he froze with his finger on the trigger.

He said, "That ain't necessary. That there's a double-action, it don't need recocking. I seen it in Thorson's shop."

"I didn't want to chance your not knowing that. The rifle." I held out my empty hand.

He stalled as long as you're supposed to in his situation, then extended the weapon butt first shamefacedly, like a boy handing over his slingshot to a sharp-eyed schoolmaster.

"Nice," I said, balancing it on top of my wrist. "What is it?"

"English. The Marquis gave it to me."

I looked it over and lowered it to the throat of my saddle. "I know you're doing your job, but I don't like rifles pointing at me from horseback. You never know when the animal might jar your finger on the trigger. Let's go talk to your boss." I holstered the revolver.

He swung the yellow horse around and started walking. I left the road to follow. At length I spied my badge gleaming in the grass and leaned down to pick it up. There was a dent between two of the points where my bullet had glanced off, not its first.

CHAPTER 10

"You need those glasses?"

We had been riding side by side for half an hour. The scenery hadn't changed and the silence, together with the constant hammocking between the rolling hills, was stultifying. I'd about given up on getting an answer when he said, "Beats walking into doors."

"Don't they get in the way of the little holes?"

He turned that over and studied it from both sides before responding. "Holes?"

"The ones you cut in the pillowcase to see through while you're wearing it. It's a mystery to me how you can see to sling a rope over a branch. Or are you the one that holds the horse?"

Our mounts' fetlocks swished through the grass, the only sound for miles. He was either slow or cautious. I had my money on the latter. "You been talking to Pardee."

I shook my head. "His mind is made up it's Mather's men doing the harassing. I think it's spread around a little more than that."

"Don't believe I'll say anything more."

"About time, chatterbox."

Two hours out of Breen we topped a rise higher than most and the framework of a huge building sprang into view atop a graded hill on the horizon. It was taller than it was wide, towering forty feet over the ranch house sprawled an acre away. The outbuildings in between looked like children's scattered

blocks. Here and there across the rippled vastness that separated the Big and Little Belt Mountains, cattle grazed alone
and in clumps. Squinting, I could just make out men crawling
over the half-finished roof of the skeletal structure like ter-
mites.

"That's some barn your boss is building," I commented.

"Barn, hell." For once he spoke without hesitation. "That's
his new headquarters."

"What's he need a castle for way out here?"

"He calls it a chateau." It came out "shat-oo."

A couple of lanky cowhands were leaning on the corral
fence, smoking and watching as a third sidled up to a black
mare in the enclosure with a coil of rope in hand, making kiss-
ing noises to calm the skittish animal. The pair turned their
heads to follow our progress to the ranch house. They were
young, but their faces were brown and cracked at the corners
of their eyes and mouths from months of squinting against
harsh sunlight.

As we neared the long front porch, a maple block of a man
came out and rested the barrel of a Remington rolling-block
rifle on the porch railing. He was dressed in colorless jeans
and a red-and-white plaid shirt that had bled pink from too
many scrubbings.

"Who we got, Arnie?" His pleasant baritone didn't go with
the steel in his eyes. Hatless, he was bald to the crown, but
the blond handlebar that swung below his cheeks more than
made up for the dearth of hair topside. He looked forty and
was probably closer to thirty.

"Who's got who is open to question." I held up Arnie's English rifle. "Just for the record, though, the name's Murdock."

He studied me. "I heard you was mean-looking. You don't
look like such a much to me."

"That's what a good night's sleep will do for you. Is he in?"

"To you maybe. Not to all that iron."

76

I thrust the foreign rifle into Arnie's hands. He flushed beneath the older man's angry gaze.

"Sorry, Uncle Ed."

There was a brief silence, and then the other's face clouded suddenly and he clomped off the porch carrying the Remington, reached up and wrenched the English gun out of Arnie's grasp by its barrel. The pretty horse flinched snorting and backed up a step. Its master looked even more frightened.

"You just let two men take it away from you in one afternoon." The blocky man was breathing heavily, his chest pumping as if from a great effort. "You'll get it back when you learn to hang on to it."

I said, "Do you do that often?"

"Do what?" He was still glaring at the abashed youth.

"Grab a loaded rifle by the muzzle and yank. I knew a deputy sheriff who used to do that with pistols. He's got a pretty widow."

He grunted and turned away, carrying the rifles at his sides like buckets of slop. As he walked he swung his left leg in a half-circle without bending the knee. The limp was more noticeable when he wasn't in a hurry. "Wait here." At the door he turned to nail Arnie again. "You tell Kruger to get someone else to ride line. Man can't drive off rustlers without no gun." The door banged in its casing.

The boy pressed his thick lips tight and wheeled, kicking yard mud over my roan's flanks as he cantered off toward the long low bunkhouse on the other side of the corral. I dismounted and hitched up to the porch railing. The man with the handlebar came out while I was yanking the tie. He was still carrying the Remington, but he had ditched the foreign piece.

"He'll talk."

I stepped onto the porch. "Lead the way, Uncle Ed."

"Name's Strayhorn." He braced his right foot on the threshold and vaulted the other up and over.

We passed through a shallow entrance hall into a large room with a redwood floor and two large windows in the south wall made of rows of eight-inch-square panes that let in plenty of light. Quilted-leather chairs squatted around a fireplace of whitewashed stone big enough for a man to crouch in. Above the mantel, a painting of Napoleon I on horseback scowled from a heavy gold frame, but aside from that, there was nothing French about the room save its owner.

The Marquis was standing in gartered shirtsleeves and a red silk vest to the right of the fireplace with his hands clasped behind his back like a St. Louis shoe clerk and Arnie's rifle on a low mahogany table in front of him. His forelock and pointed whiskers looked even more preposterous in these surroundings than they had in my hotel room.

"Dear me, you have had an accident," he observed.

I'd forgotten about the cheek scratches. "I'll live."

"In my country, marks like those are considered a measure of one's manhood."

"In my country they're considered evidence of rape."

"Oh, but they are not so deep as that. Perhaps just a little rape. Thank you, Edward."

It was a dismissal, but Strayhorn hesitated. "I still think I should take his gun."

"Nonsense. Assassination is not Monsieur Murdock's way." His tone held a sarcastic edge. The other man raked his hard eyes over me as he limped out, still holding the buffalo gun.

"That's a fine rifle," I ventured, nodding at the weapon on the table. "Balanced like a clock."

He picked it up and cradled it lovingly. In his small hands it looked like a cannon. "It is a Martini light four hundred, presented to me by the Empress Eugénie at the time I left Europe. At one hundred yards it has a striking energy of one thousand four hundred and forty-three foot-pounds. It is the only thing of any worth that the English have ever produced, and it comes as no surprise that it was designed by an Italian. The first Napoleon was Italian, you know."

"As I recall, it was an Englishman who defeated him."

"Well, you have not come to discuss history." He replaced the rifle with a startling noise. I had drawn blood.

"I met Pardee last night," I said. "Terwilliger's foreman. He swears neither he nor his boss sent for Chris Shedwell."

"Were I in their position, I would swear as much."

"I believe him."

"My compliments. Your faith in your fellow man is to be admired, if not imitated."

"His reasoning was sound. Why were he and his men in town last night to start something with Mather if he'd arranged for Shedwell to balance the account?"

"Then perhaps you can tell me why he is coming?" When I didn't answer he frowned exaggeratedly, pushing out his lips. "Let us say, just for the sake of argument, that Monsieur Terwilliger has not engaged Monsieur Shedwell's talents and that he is coming only to visit his dear mother, assuming that he has one. How does that change anything? The small ranchers continue to swell their herds at the expense of their larger neighbors."

"How can you be sure they've been rustling Six Bar Six cattle?"

"It is not just Mather's misfortune. The spring roundup has begun, and already the tallies are falling behind estimates. We expect a loss of a thousand calves. Perhaps more."

"Estimates based on book count," I said. "We may be talking about calves that never existed."

"It would be a very large error, would it not? Unpardonable."

"Even if you're right, that's a lot of rustling for one man. He wouldn't have any time left to run his ranch."

"He is not the only small rancher in the territory, monsieur. I do not claim that he alone is responsible for the loss. But he is the leader."

"Let's talk straight," I said. "It wouldn't matter if not one calf came up missing or if you found a thousand more than you estimated. You'd just find some other way to justify clearing out the small fry and claiming the open range for yourself."

I had raised my voice without realizing it. Now I heard footsteps behind me and turned to see Ed Strayhorn standing in front of the door with his ever-present Remington in both hands. I backed away at an angle, resting my right hand on the Deane-Adams.

"Call off your foreman."

"Bookkeeper," Périgueux corrected. "The leg, you see. But it does not hinder his aim. Please leave."

"Not until I've said what I came to say. Last night I made a deal with Pardee to let me handle the situation my way. I was going to cut you in, but since you're not interested, I'll say this: if Terwilliger or Pardee or any of their men is hurt or killed while I'm marshal, even if it's from falling off a horse— hell, even if it's from smallpox—I'll know right where to go. And I'll have help."

"Are you finished?" asked the Frenchman, after a pause.

"Not quite. I need directions to Terwilliger's spread. I want to ask Dale Pardee about some night riders that have been bothering him lately. You wouldn't know anything about that."

"I have heard rumors." He pointed at a framed parchment map on the west wall. It was shaped roughly like a water jug with a chipped neck. "That is my ranch, and that"—he indicated the missing piece—"is the Circle T, belonging to Monsieur Terwilliger, twelve miles west by northwest."

"That must be like a splinter in your ear."

"It itches from time to time. *Au revoir*, Monsieur Murdock. That means—"

"I know what it means." I shouldered my way past Strayhorn.

CHAPTER 11

I hadn't time to ride to the Circle T, interview Pardee's brother, and get back to town before nightfall, so I postponed that trip until morning. Night was the time when all hell broke loose in cattle towns. A mile out of Breen I got out the bottle I'd brought in my saddlebag from Helena for the cold nights and drained the eighth of an inch of colored liquid left in the bottom. The temperature had hovered around thirty most nights, and as I said before it was a long ride. I swung out of the saddle and set up the empty on the spine of a low ridge. It was time I found out how much I could expect from the new gun.

I rode out forty yards, dismounted again, passed the Deane-Adams up and down the length of my sleeve just to hear the cylinder clack around and took aim at the neck of the bottle while the roan, ground-trained but pretending not to be, wandered off after new grass. Sunlight glared off the smooth glass, but I didn't change my angle. It glares off a man's belt buckle the same way, and he isn't likely to wait while you find a better location.

I stood sideways to the target because I'm harder to hit that way, sighting down the length of my outstretched arm the way they don't in the dime novels, and was squeezing the trigger when the bottle separated into two pieces with a hollow plop. The neck and the base tilted away from each other like halves of a wishbone, and then the shot crashed, its echo retreating toward the mountains like rumbling thunder. I hit

81

the ground for the third time in two days and rolled behind a clump of bramble.

After half a minute I used the barrel of the revolver to part the brush and peered out. To the west, a man on horseback nosed a carbine into a before-the-knee scabbard, smacked his reins across the animal's withers, and came galloping straight at me.

The sun at his back was blinding. Squinting, I hunkered down with my shooting arm resting straight out in the bramble's crotch and waited for him to move into pistol range.

A hundred yards off he reined in and leaned on his fists on the pommel of his saddle. He wore a linen duster over a town suit and his face was in shadow beneath the brim of a black hat I thought I'd seen before.

"Murdock," he called, his voice rising and falling on the prairie wind, "you are a one for lying down in the middle of the afternoon."

"You son of a bitch," I muttered in relief. But I held onto the revolver. Raising my voice: "Yardlinger, you are a one for asking to get your moustache shot off."

"Not unless that gun Thorson sold you fires Sharps Big Fifty cartridges."

I got up, holding it at hip level. Sometimes it pays to look like you walked out of something by Ned Buntline. "Step down and start leading your horse this way. From the left side, opposite the scabbard. I'll tell you when to stop. And keep your hand away from your belt gun."

He was quiet for a moment. "You don't set much store by friends."

"I had a friend once," I said. "He tried to gut me with a skinning knife when I beat his straight with a full house. Move."

He did as directed, leading his piebald by the bit and holding his left arm straight out to the side like a carpenter carrying a heavy toolbox in the other hand. The rifle on the saddle was the Winchester carbine I'd carried the night before. When he was fifty feet away I motioned him with the revolver to stop.

"Now neither of us has to shout." I relaxed a little, resting the butt of the Deane-Adams on the bone of my hip. "Start with why you shattered that bottle."

"Is that all that's biting you?" He smiled, but it died short of his eyes. "I never could resist a target like that. I'm the champion rifle shot of the county three years running."

I watched him, especially his eyes. At length I sighed and replaced the revolver in its holster. "It was a hell of a good shot." I wanted to say something more, to try and restore the good thing that had been growing between us. Instead I said, "What are you doing out here?"

"Looking for you." His tone was colder than it had been when we'd met. "Pardee rolled into town an hour ago on a buckboard. His brother's in the back. Someone lynched him, and this time they finished the job."

We found the buckboard in front of one of the town's two undertaking parlors. The box was empty but for a coil of rotted twine and about a pound of wet sawdust, wagon stuff. BYRON C. FITCH, MORTICIAN was lettered in gold paint across the parlor's curtained front window.

The interior of the parlor looked more like a cathouse than most cathouses I'd seen. Curtains were drawn across the front window and lamplight sifted dimly over the muted carpet and rows of mourners' chairs arranged in front of a casket on a raised platform draped in black felt. The sweet smell of hothouse-grown flowers enveloped us as we entered.

An old man with wispy white hair brushed back over dry pink scalp and a scowl that had defied the undertaker's best efforts lay in the casket, his head raised on a satin pillow and spotted hands folded across his vest. We took off our hats, as if that mattered any more, and went on past him through a door standing half open into the back room.

Rosy light from the setting sun fell through two small windows high in the west wall, illuminating a cluttered pine bench, half a dozen lidless caskets, and a naked corpse stretched out on a pair of planks nailed together and propped across a pair of sawhorses. The raw stench of formaldehyde contrasted sharply with the flowery smell in the parlor.

A pudgy man in shirtsleeves who had been bent over the body glanced up and said, "Thank God! Please help Mr. Pardee out of here, Marshal. He's not doing anyone any good, especially himself." I recognized him as the man I had seen riding shotgun on Marshal Arno's hearse the day before.

Pardee, in rusty range clothes and a Stetson grown colorless from sweat and weather, looked like a man on the wrong end of a long fever. His face was slack and heavy, his eyes hot and sunk deep in purple-black sockets. I almost didn't recognize him without a cigar.

"Look at him." His voice was so low he might have been praying. "Look at what those bastards did to him." He was gazing at the thing on the planks.

The dead man was whipsaw-lean, tanned from neck to hairline and from fingers to wrists, and gray-white everywhere else. His eyes bulged, the burst blood vessels in the whites black and twisted like hairs on the lip of a washbasin, and his tongue was a dark swollen thing that had grown too big for his mouth to hold. The rope had burned a blue line around his neck and the weight of his body had stretched it twice its normal length. His clothes had been flung to the floor in a heap.

"Pardee said he was last seen this morning, when he rode north after some strays," Yardlinger said. "When he didn't show up by midafternoon, Pardee and some of the hands went looking for him. They found him dangling from a tree a mile inside the Circle T's northwest corner."

"A mile short of the Six Bar Six." The foreman's prayerful moan had fallen to a hoarse whisper. "They didn't even bother to tie much of a knot. They just let him strangle."

"Whose strays was he after?" I asked. "Terwilliger's or Mather's?"

Yardlinger gaped. "Murdock, for God's sake—"

But Pardee was already moving. In one spring he was on me, his big muscular hands squeezing my throat. His eyes bulged like his dead brother's and saliva foamed at the corner of his mouth. I scooped out the Deane-Adams and pronged the barrel deep into the arch of his rib cage. Air whooshed out his lungs, spittle flecking my face. But he held on. My vision turned black around the edges.

I was about to fire when there was a solid *thunk* like an axe sinking into soft wood; Pardee's eyes rolled over white, his hands clutched at my shoulders for support when his grip failed on my throat. I stepped back and he toppled forward, first onto his knees and then onto his hands, where he stayed with his head hanging down.

Yardlinger was standing over him, holding his Navy Colt like a hammer with the butt foremost. When he was sure the foreman's part in the drama was finished he executed a neat spin that ended with the gun securely in its holster.

"Obliged. Not that I needed help." I put up my own gun the conventional way.

"He was in the right. That was a hell of a thing to say."

"Maybe. If those strays had turned out to be Mather's, I'd have known where to look for his brother's killer."

"That won't be a problem."

"Mather strikes me as smarter than that, knowing we'd suspect him. Unless some of his hands decided to do the boss a favor on their own time."

"That's Turk all over."

The undertaker was agitated. "Quick, Marshal, get Mr. Pardee out of here. He makes me nervous."

"I can see why," said the deputy. "Your customers don't usually comment on your work." He'd been watching Pardee, who remained in a daze on his hands and knees. Now Yardlinger looked at the little man. "He had five men with him when I left. Where'd they go?"

The undertaker shrugged distractedly. "They went out right after helping carry in the body."

I said, "Twenty dollars on where they're going," and started walking.

Yardlinger called after me. "It'll be dark in a few minutes. You'll break your neck."

"That'll save Judge Blackthorne the trouble when he hears I let a range war blow up in my jurisdiction. I'll fetch the other deputies. Lock up Pardee and wait for us at the jail." I scattered empty chairs on my way through the parlor.

CHAPTER 12

We clattered down the freezing, shadow-splashed street at full gallop, five men on wild-eyed horses loaded down with iron, a hellish sight for the curious who had come out to see what the commotion was about. Of the two rifles left in the rack I had chosen a Henry for myself and made Cross give up his shotgun for a Spencer. Yardlinger, who held on to the Winchester, informed me that Earl and the Major knew their way around handguns well enough to do without. The old man, who had no horse of his own, had commandeered one from the livery. Our destination was the Six Bar Six.

Clouds boiled past the moon, merging the solid black of trees lining the road with the smothering wrap of the night itself. The horses were frightened and let us know with whinnies drawn thin as threads of molten silver. Vapor billowed from their nostrils. The air was as cold as the water in a mountain stream.

Yardlinger rode point as guide. At first I had nothing to go by but the feel of his piebald's back-drifting breath on my face, but as my eyes caught up with the darkness I was able to make out his lanky form in the saddle. Now all I had to worry about was the occasional chuckhole in the road, which could splinter a horse's cannon like green wood.

Time stands still at night. It might have been five minutes and it might have been an hour before we heard a crackling in the distance, as of someone crumpling brittle parchment. There was no telling from which direction the sound of the shots had come. I slowed to a canter and finally to a walk, barking at the others to do the same.

"What we doglegging for?" Earl wanted to know. "You got a bet on how it'll come out?"

I ignored the sneer in his tone. "We won't get there any faster on dead horses."

"He's right. Shut up," said Yardlinger.

We alternated between cantering and walking while the animals' sides heaved and their spent breath enveloped us in a shroud of moist warmth. Meanwhile, the distant crackling continued in fits and starts, now pausing, now erupting again in flurries so rapid it was impossible to count the individual reports. It sounded unreal, like fake gunfire onstage.

The horses smelled it first and passed it along to us in exhausted snorts and the dozen other noises they make when approaching a place of rest after a hard ride. It reached us a moment later. I stood in the stirrups and drew in a double lungful of the familiar, faintly pleasant odor redolent of hundreds of nights spent around stoves and campfires. Woodsmoke. I was about to call it to the others' attention when Yardlinger grunted and I looked ahead to see a red glow fanning out across the western sky.

I'd seen something like it once before, riding with Rosecrans' cavalry on the way to hell at Murfreesboro. Coming out of a patch of woods, we had spotted the fires of a Confederate encampment reflected in the low-hanging clouds six miles away. It looked like the sun getting ready to rise, and it only happened when there was a lot of flame . . .

We pushed our mounts the rest of the way. Even so, we were a long time getting there, too long. We heard men shouting and horses screaming and more shots raggedly spaced, and then we heard nothing but the splitting and popping of wood being consumed by fire. *Too late,* said the hoofbeats beneath us. *Too late, too late.* Then we thundered over a rise and were there.

88

The blaze had passed its peak, but coming straight from darkness I had to shield my eyes against the glare. Flames were slurping at the charred framework of what had been a large barn, clinging to the corner beams, and crouching along the rafters like hordes of magpies stuffing their swollen bellies long after the carcass had been reduced to gristle and bone. An occasional horseman flashed past and was swallowed up in darkness. There was galloping around us, two or three shots fired at nothing in particular, and then there was nothing at all, just the noise of the fire sating itself. I spurred the roan in that direction, fighting it all the way.

"Murdock! Stay back!" Yardlinger's voice was strident. "The barn's coming down!"

The heat on my face was blistering. My mount fought the bit and reared. I threw all my weight onto its neck, and when its forefeet touched ground I swung out of the saddle, landing flat on my heels with a jar that sent sharp pains splintering up my legs. The roan nearly knocked me down with its shoulder as it spun to get clear of the flames and smoke.

Yellow tongues lapped and stuttered at the doomed wood, flicking illumination this way and that. I was alerted to a chilling sound nearby, half snort and half whistling whimper, and saw a horse kicking and thrashing on its side in the barn's blazing doorway, a mass of charred, flaming flesh still fighting for life. Its eyes were gone and its lips had burned away to expose grotesquely leering teeth. I put a bullet in its head from the Deane-Adams. It arched its neck and flopped to the ground like a trout landing, emptying its lungs with a sigh and thrusting its legs in four directions.

The air next to my right ear split with a sharp crack, simultaneous with the deep report. On the edge of the firelight leaned a wagon with a broken wheel; in the right triangle of darkness beneath I spotted a blue phosphorescence on the fade and fired at it, darting for shadow even as I loosed the

89

shot. I waited, but no bullets answered. Instead I heard a voice.

"Don't shoot! I'm wounded."

It was a young voice, breathless and cracking.

I said, "Can you stand?"

I heard grunting and struggling. A pause. "No."

Major Brody was standing just beyond the circle of light, which glinted orange off his Peacemaker's sight. "Cover him," I snapped.

"You bet, Cap'n." He cackled shortly. "Don't make no moves I might regard as hostile, young feller. I'm mostly owl and a little bit bat. That means I can see in the dark."

I circled around and came up on the wagon's blind side, stifling a curse when I tripped over a bulky object on the ground and almost fell. It was a man's body. I bent down, groped for his collar, and pressed my fingers against the big artery on the side of his neck. It was just a useless tube now. I crept around the corpse.

As I drew near the wagon, the flames found an unburned section of rafter and flared up greedily, lighting the space under the broken-down vehicle. The man lay on his left hip, his left arm stretched out along the ground ending in a revolver and his right leg thrust in the opposite direction. His pants leg was slick with blood where he was gripping it with his free right hand. His face was turned toward the Major.

When the light died, I took two long strides and, going by memory, stuck my left foot under the wagon on top of his gun arm and reached sideways and down to clap the muzzle of my revolver to his temple. He stiffened, then struggled to free the trapped arm, but I leaned into it and he gave up.

"Please don't shoot me, mister," he begged again. "I think my leg's busted."

Brody spoke up. "Who's your boss? Turk or Pardee?"

There was no answer. The old man spat. I heard the tobacco splatter the wagon's sideboards. "You called it, son."

"Don't shoot!" I put as much authority into the command as I could muster. The old night rider was in his element and I wasn't sure he could be controlled. "Not unless you want to swing right here."

It made him pause. Skeptically: "You'd do that? A U.S. marshal?"

"Deputy," I corrected. "And you're damn right."

Some more time passed. Finally I heard the slide and click of the Colt's hammer being replaced. Going into his belt the gun made a creaking sound like tightly gloved fingers curling into a fist.

I said, "Fix up some kind of torch and bring it here."

We were left in darkness for several minutes. The wounded man's breath moved in and out sibilantly, fluttering from time to time and catching whenever a spasm of pain shot through him. I heard Yardlinger shouting to Earl and Cross to check out each of the other outbuildings, neither of which had been touched by fire. It was like listening to an argument in the next hotel room, of interest to me but none of my business.

I was beginning to wonder what had happened to the Major when a ball of flame separated from the dying blaze of the barn and bobbed our way, his bowlegged figure hobbling beneath it. At that moment the roof fell in with a noise like a bundle of laundry striking the floor from a great height. Bright orange sparks swarmed upward for a hundred feet and vanished. A corner post tilted, hung motionless for a couple of seconds, and toppled away from the inferno, crunching when it struck ground. Brody didn't even turn to watch. I guessed he'd seen his share of burning buildings.

"I soaked a loose stave in a barrel of coal oil I found back of the barn," he said, squatting to grin at us from the other side of the wagon. His stubbly face was smeared black with soot.

"What do you want," I retorted, "a Johnny Reb medal? Hold it steady."

He cackled again. I never found out if he did that out of habit or for effect. "I still like you."

The wounded man was one of the horseback riders we'd confronted with Mather in Breen the night before. I pried his Navy Colt out of his grasp, stuck it in my belt and lifted my boot from his wrist. He rubbed it with his other hand, bloody from nursing his own wound.

"I'm Murdock." I leathered the Deane-Adams. "You remember me."

He looked at me, blankly at first, and then he nodded. He had brown hair and pimples. "I remember. I thought you was one of them bushwhackers. That's why—" He sucked air through his teeth and gripped his leg.

"Let's have a look at that."

I got down on one knee and gently lifted his hand from the pants leg, stiff with gore and glistening in the torchlight. "Got a knife?"

The Major handed me his, a slasher with a hide-wrapped hilt. I used it to slit the material from knee to thigh and pulled it apart. Bits of white bone showed in a wound as big as a doorknob. I covered it hurriedly.

"It's broken." I didn't tell him how badly. "We'll get help."

"Help's here."

I looked up. A man was standing behind the Major with his back to the flames and a lever-action rifle in both hands, trained on us. Brody dropped the torch and went for the revolver in his belt.

"I'll blow your heart out the wrong side." The deep voice was so calm there was almost no threat to it. Almost. It sounded familiar, but I'd heard too many new voices in the past couple of days to sort them out. The Major let his hand drop from the Peacemaker's butt.

"Who is it?" I demanded.

"Turk."

"It's all right, Abel," broke in the wounded boy. "They ain't with the bushwhackers."

"Then whose bullet is that in your leg?"

There was no answer.

I said, "He fired at me. I fired back. I didn't know if he was with you or Terwilliger."

"Terwilliger." Turk dragged out the name, giving each syllable more than its full value. "I figured it was him."

"I don't know that he was with them. They're friends of Pardee's. Someone lynched his brother today. I don't guess you'd know who."

"You ain't in a position to be asking questions." The rifle barrel was a foot away from my head.

"I'm not in a position to do much of anything, least of all save your cowhand's life. He'll bleed to death if you don't let Brody pick up that torch so I can finish what I started."

The fire crackled behind him. "All right, go ahead. Just don't move too fast."

"Mister, I got to move fast." When the torch was lifted, I took the kerchief from around my neck and twisted it around the boy's thigh just above the leaking wound. The bleeding slowed. "Where can we take him? Someplace with a bed and not too many stairs to climb."

"The main house," said Turk. "I'll fetch help."

He left, to return a few minutes later with four men in faded denims and bulky cowhide jackets, two of them carrying something that looked like a door. I placed one of them among those I had seen in town last night. The others were strangers.

"The door's from the coal shed," the foreman explained. "We can use it for a litter."

It was slid under the wagon next to the boy and two men took positions on either side. The boy gasped during the transfer but didn't cry out. Meanwhile I supported the leg, and when the litter was slid out into the open and lifted, I went along to hold the tourniquet while the Major bore the torch and Turk led the way.

I kept the boy talking to keep his mind off the pain. He explained that the ambushers had struck while the hands were on their way to the bunkhouse for supper, firing the barn and hurling lead at the men as they scattered for cover.

The main house was a big log structure a couple of hundred yards west of the smoldering shell of a barn. No attempt had been made to disguise the logs, which brought up my opinion of Dick Mather ten percent. The Major ditched the torch and we carefully levered our burden around a shallow, L-shaped entryway and through a spacious room with a sputtering fire and Indian rugs on the walls into a small ground-floor bedroom. A stout woman in a plain blouse and floor-length floral skirt made way for us, babbling away in bastardized French. That, together with her dark round face and flat Indian features, identified her as one of the half-breed Canadians who supplied most of the domestic labor in the region.

We set the improvised litter down on the floor next to the bed while the woman peeled back the heavy counterpane. Then we lifted him onto the mattress, me keeping his leg from flopping. He cursed beneath his breath while the spread was tucked around his chin.

"Fetch Tom Petit," Turk barked. The man thus addressed left.

"Is Petit a doctor?"

The foreman looked at me. Indoors, his hat low over his sloping forehead so that the V of the brim almost touched the broken hump of his nose, he looked more primitive than ever. His eyes were hooded under his low brow. "He was a medic in the war. Now he works for the Six Bar Six. He's the closest thing we got to a doctor this side of town." He jerked his chin toward the bed. "I don't think he can wait for the ride there and back."

I left the tourniquet to another's care and caught up with the cowhand he'd dispatched at the front door.

"Tell Petit to bring whatever he uses to cut with."

He hesitated, then nodded and went out. Yardlinger passed him coming in. His face was streaked with soot and sweat and his clothes smelled of woodsmoke. The Winchester hung loose at his side. I didn't like his expression.

"What's wrong?"

"Earl's hurt." His voice was raspy, either from yelling or from the smoke.

"Bad?"

"It doesn't get any worse."

We hurried out together.

CHAPTER 13

The barn was a tangle of beams that crossed each other and tilted out from the foundation. Flames continued to flicker in spots, but for the most part everything had burned away that could. Earl lay on his back in the wavering light, pinned to the ground by a charred beam twenty feet long lying across his midsection. His chest bellowed in and out amid breathless cursing. Cross was kneeling beside him, cradling Earl's head in his lap and repeating something I didn't catch over and over beneath his breath. His Spencer lay in the tall grass a few feet away.

"He was walking past the barn when it came down," Yardlinger whispered. "He heard it and tried to get out of the way, but he slipped and fell. He's all busted up."

"Help me."

I looked at Cross. His seamed cheeks were slick. "Give me a hand and let's get this thing off him. We got to get him to a doctor."

Still whispering, Yardlinger said, "That's another thing. One of the wooden pegs they put barns together with is sticking in his belly. We'd gut him like a fish if we tried lifting the beam."

"Poor dumb bastard." Major Brody gazed sadly at the heaving figure. I hadn't realized he'd followed us from the house until he'd spoken. "We best dig a hole right here. He'll mess up something terrible, we try to tote him back to town."

Cross cursed and lunged for his rifle. I backhanded the

Major across the face with the Deane-Adams, sending him sprawling, and stepped between them to level the gun at Cross. He froze with his hand on the weapon, then let go, one finger at a time. He settled back on his heels, rocking to and fro with Earl's head in his lap and murmuring gently.

The Major sat on the ground rubbing his bleeding cheek. "What in hell did you hit me for?" he groaned. "He was the one going for iron."

"He wouldn't have gone for it if you rode herd on your big mouth. Next time I'll put a bit in it." I stashed the gun and turned to Yardlinger. "They've got medical help up at the house. Tell him to slap a bandage on the boy's leg for now and come out here."

"He needs a shovel, not a doctor." But he retraced his steps to the house.

"You hear that, Earl?" Cross was saying. "Help's coming. We'll get you fixed up in no time."

The young deputy didn't hear him. His back was arched and his mouth worked, air moving in and out shallowly. Blood bubbled in his nostrils.

I bent over the Major, now supporting himself on one elbow. "I didn't think they were that close."

"Closer'n two toes in a tight boot." He spoke petulantly, holding his handkerchief to the injured cheek. "Earl's old man used to take turns betwixt whaling him and his ma. One time he busted the kid's head with a horse collar. Randy seen it and used a quirt on the old man. Him and Earl been together since."

"Where's that goddamn doctor?" Cross was looking at me, but his eyes were out of focus. Distractedly he lowered them to the boy and stroked his pale yellow hair. Earl began to hiccough, the spasm jerking him. Suddenly his shoulders lifted and his head snapped back, tearing a keening cry from his throat, like the horse had made before I put it out of its misery. For an instant he froze in that position, and then he

98

sank back down and his head lolled to one side. His eyes and mouth remained open.

"That's the ticket," Cross said. "Rest. Save your strength."

"Randy, he's gone." It didn't sound like my voice.

"He ain't." He resumed rocking and petting. "Where's that goddamn doctor?"

In the background, charred wood hissed and popped as it cooled. Beams and rafters glowed in sections, looking like the snakeweed we used to pull apart and put back together as kids. Major Brody got up grunting.

Moments later Yardlinger returned, flanked by a short man wearing a sheepskin coat and a Buffalo Bill beard and carrying a black leather satchel scuffed brown at the edges. Randy looked up at him like a Mexican gazing at a plaster saint.

"He hurts bad, Doc."

"Not any more he don't." Petit—I supposed it was him—glanced from the corpse to me. "You the one sent for medical help?" I nodded. "You look like you should know a dead'un when you see him."

"He wasn't dead when I sent for you."

"Dead or dying, it adds up the same. I got to get back to someone I can save. You been busy tonight." He turned away.

Cross leaped across Earl's still form and spun him around by the shoulder. The Spencer was in his hand.

"What the hell kind of a doctor are you?" He was shouting, waving the muzzle under Petit's nose. "We got a man here needs patching!"

The former medic's eyes sought mine. Sad eyes, calm as a toad's. "He always like this?"

"He's pretty shaken up."

"I noticed that. Can you call him off?"

I held back. Cross had the rifle cocked and his finger rested on the trigger. I didn't want to startle him into spraying Petit's brains all over western Montana. The barn's abused timbers groaned and spat. Then the weapon drooped in Cross's hands and he started to cry. I reached out and gently twisted the Spencer out of his grasp.

"Obliged," said Petit and continued on his way.

I took the rifle off cock and handed it to Yardlinger. "Think you and the Major can undo Earl from that beam?"

"I think so. It isn't all that heavy. A few more pounds on the sunny side and it might only have—"

"And if the barn were made of steel it wouldn't have fallen at all. Wrap Earl in his saddle blanket and sling him over his horse. Bring the animals up to the main house when you're through."

"What are you going to do?" he asked.

"Pay my respects to the host."

I returned to the bedroom in time to hear Petit ask Turk for laudanum. The foreman turned to the woman half-breed and said something in halting French. She replied, shrugging. Turk turned back.

"There ain't none."

"Whiskey, then."

At "whiskey," the woman's face brightened and a stream of rapid French followed. In the middle of it Turk said, "Three bottles."

"Tell her to get them. All of them."

She hurried out, her skirt scuffing the floor.

The foreman watched Petit open his satchel. "Think that's a good idea? I hear drinking that much in a short time can kill a man."

"There are worse ways to die. Besides, some of it's for me."

By this time the boy in the bed had given up any pretense of bravery and was exhaling curses, his voice rising to a shriek whenever the pain grew acute. His trousers had been cut away and his bare leg lay atop the counterpane with a temporary bandage wound around the gaping hole in his thigh. My kerchief had been replaced by a clean white rag knotted loosely above the wound, the ends left out for quick tightening. Petit did nothing to make the patient more comfortable. I guessed that was so the boy wouldn't notice the instruments the former medic was taking from his satchel and laying side by side on the table next to the bed. The hacksaw's teeth looked sharp enough to shave with.

"Go outside," Turk told the four men who had helped carry in the boy. "Find out how many men we lost."

"Not yet." Petit held the saw over a chipped enamel basin and drenched the blade with liquid from a pint bottle. A hospital stench flooded the room. "They'll be needed."

"For what?"

He left the saw soaking in alcohol and rammed the cork back into the bottle. "Because whiskey is a rotten anesthetic."

"Christ's sake, Tom, you don't mean you're really—"

"I'm a cowhand, not a surgeon." His face darkened. "I don't know the first thing about piecing them slivers back together and neither does Doc Ballard in Breen. That leg'll start mortifying tomorrow. You know how fast gangrene travels? Two inches every hour. It's coming off."

"*No!*"

The boy's hoarse scream buzzed in the rafters. He seized Turk's sleeve. His face was gray, the whites of his eyes luminous by contrast. "Abel, don't let him take my leg. How'll I sit a horse?"

The foreman smiled uncomfortably and blustered, "Nothing to it, Jim. We'll whittle you one of them pegs and you'll be bouncing around like a jackrabbit in no time. Hell, you can tell the girls you lost it fighting injuns. They'll be all over you."

"No peg," Petit said. "Not when it's above the knee."

The lamp hissed on the table.

"Abel." Jim's grip tightened on the older man's arm. "If you let him cut it off I'll shoot myself in the head. If you hide every gun on the Six Bar Six I'll cut my throat. If you throw away my razor I'll set myself on fire with that there lamp. You can have someone watching me all the time, but he's got to take his eyes off me once, and that's when I'll do it."

The woman returned with the three bottles of liquor. Turk took one and yanked the cork with his teeth. "Have a pull, Jim," he said, spitting it out. "It'll make you feel better."

For a moment the boy's gaze remained on the foreman. Then he released Turk's sleeve as if throwing it away and seized the bottle. As he upended it, Petit leaned across the bed and whispered: "Leave me the four men and clear out. I need room to work."

"You going to be able to handle him?" Turk sounded dubious.

"That's what the four men are for."

Turk nodded toward the boy, who was choking from the whiskey. "You reckon he meant what he said? About killing himself?"

Petit glanced uneasily at Jim and slid his hand under Turk's arm, drawing him away from the bed. The bottle made plopping noises as the patient tipped it up again.

"I must of helped the surgeons lop off arms and legs a hundred times in the war," whispered the medic. "Maybe fifteen of them lived. It wasn't on account of blood loss or gangrene or even fever, though they all got that. They just didn't want to. I don't think he'll last long enough to kill himself."

"Well then, why in hell bother, if he's going to die anyway?" He was almost choking with the urge to shout. Petit shushed him.

"I asked the surgeons the same thing. They said it wasn't their job to stand by and watch a man die. If it wasn't theirs, it sure as hell ain't mine."

He straightened, looking like a doctor. "Leave Clarice here with the hands. I'll need a nurse."

"Where's Mather?" I asked Turk, in the living room.

He snatched my collar and gathered it up in both fists. An

inch shorter, he glared up at me. His beard bristled and his eyes were bloodshot.

"I lost three men tonight, not counting that boy. One was in the barn when a bushwhacker's bullet busted a lantern and he burned to death with six horses. Two more to gunshots. There might be more. I been kind of distracted. If you'd let me settle with Pardee last night in town, none of it would of happened. Give me one good reason why I shouldn't bust your neck."

"I'll give you five," I said. "At this range, any one of them would do the job."

He glanced down. In his rage he'd failed to notice the Deane-Adams prodding him in the belly. He let me go with a shove.

I put the gun away and handed him the Colt I'd taken from Jim. "I wouldn't give it to him for a while. What happens now?"

He rotated the cylinder, inspecting the rounds. Only one had been fired. "Now I finish what I set out to do last night."

"I can't stop you," I said. "I wouldn't try, on your own ground with only three deputies. But if one Terwilliger man dies from other than natural causes, I'll pick out a rope for you personally."

"That your kind of law?" Having put the Colt in his pocket, he was jerking spent cartridges from the cylinder of his Smith American and replacing them from his belt. Brass shells plinked to the floor. "It's all right for the small ranchers to do murder but not for the big ones to hit back?"

"If men from the Circle T killed your men and fired that barn, they'll stand trial. That much I can guarantee."

"I heard all about your guarantees. How's that deal you made with Pardee stand now?"

"Pardee's brother was murdered. I'll make an arrest on that too. The rope will decide who's right and who's wrong in this war."

He holstered the big .44. "Funny thing about ropes. The

way they stretch and snap back, you can never be sure who they'll hit."

"It's the same with bullets," I said.

"Not when you're standing behind them."

He stalked out, providing me with a fine view of his back all the way out the door. I didn't take advantage of it. I guessed I was mellowing with age.

CHAPTER 14

Alone in the greater part of the house, I eventually wandered upstairs and saw light leaking out of a door standing open in a narrow hallway. Voices were raised in argument inside. I peered in and saw Dick Mather, in flannel trousers and gray underwear top, seated on the edge of a rumpled bed struggling into calf-high boots. A solid woman in a rust-colored dress took hold of his arms to stop him, but he shook her off. His face matched the dingy, many-times-washed color of his underwear and his eyes looked swollen. He was coughing, the sound hollow and bubbling in his throat.

"Let Abel handle it," the woman pleaded. "That's what you pay him for."

"I pay him to run cattle." His words came in short bursts between wheezes as he tugged at the second boot. "I fought Indians for this land, or don't you remember? I'm damn well not going to give it up to a Michigan cherry picker like Bob Terwilliger."

"I remember," she said coldly. "That boy the Blackfeet killed was my son too."

He paused, then yanked the boot on the rest of the way and stomped his heel. "Anyway, I'm experienced at this kind of thing. Turk isn't."

"Isn't he?"

The woman started and whirled to face me, one fist flying to her mouth. Mather glanced up quickly. His lank red hair flopped into his eyes. He jerked it back with a toss of his head and dived for something under a pillow.

"I wouldn't," I said, without moving.

It made him hesitate. Arm still outstretched he said, "Just how fast are you?"

I snorted. "That again. When I came out here, fast meant women and horses. Thanks to the writers back East it's become a contest to see who can get his gun out first. I've lost that contest six or seven times. They're dead. I'm not."

It was a hell of a speech, but I'll never know if it would have worked, because he resumed coughing suddenly. He doubled over and clawed a handkerchief from his hip pocket. Meanwhile his wife leaned over the bed and plucked his derringer from under the pillow. Holding it firmly by the butt, she tugged open the top drawer of the bedside table, dropped it in and pushed the drawer shut. Her amber eyes glared at me from a strong face.

"Now you can kill us."

I looked from her to Mather, who had passed the peak of his fit and was dry-hacking into the handkerchief, his sunken chest heaving.

"Why is it you skinny guys get all the best women?"

He mopped the corners of his mouth, sat for a moment breathing heavily with his hands dangling between his knees, then returned the handkerchief to his pocket after studying it for fresh spots. "What the hell do you want?" His voice was a raspy whisper.

"Answers to a few questions. Was Turk here all day today?"

"He was out supervising the spring roundup. Why?"

"Someone decorated a tree with Pardee's brother on land belonging to the Circle T. Pardee thinks it was your men did it."

He had gotten up to take his shirt from the back of a chair.

In the middle of drawing it on, he paused. "Pardee was here tonight?" Red fever-patches appeared on his cheeks.

"He's in jail, where I put him after his brother was brought into Fitch's undertaking parlor. What about the night Dale was mock-lynched by men wearing pillowcases? Or the other times night riders hit Terwilliger's spread? Was Turk around those times?"

Mather fastened the buttons. "He may be a lot of things, but he wouldn't do his killing from behind a mask. If I thought he was that kind, I'd shoot him where he stood."

"That's the trouble. Men like you using the law when it suits their convenience and throwing it away when it doesn't are what makes men like Turk possible."

He said, "Get the hell out of here before I call him back."

"It's your house." I grasped the knob. "As someone you're throwing out I'm tempted not to give you the warning, but as peace officer for the time being I'm obliged to remind you that snakes don't always come when you call them, and when they do, they don't always bite who you want."

He seemed about to say something in response when the screaming began downstairs.

"What in sweet Jesus—!" He clawed open the drawer containing the derringer. His wife held onto his arm.

"Snakebite," I said and went out. The noise grew louder and more shrill as I descended the stairs, and soon I could make out the shouted obscenities. They were cut off with a gurgle. Someone had gagged Jim to keep him from distracting Tom Petit. But then I could hear the sawing. I barely reached the front porch in time to retch outside.

The ride back to town was quiet. Cross had trouble hanging on to the reins by which he was leading Earl's horse, but our offers of assistance were met with growls. The animal, white-eyed, its hackles standing, kept trying to bite through the ropes lashing the bundled corpse to its back and hurl it off. In front of Fitch's we dismounted to help Cross with the body. He struck away our hands, then gathered it in his arms and carried it through the front door like a father bringing his oversize exhausted son home from a picnic. We stood in the street watching as the little undertaker hastened to close the door and attend to his latest customer.

"Is Randy the kind to hold a grudge?" I asked Yardlinger.

"I don't know what kind he is. He doesn't talk much about himself or anything else for that matter. I don't even know where he came from originally or if Cross is his real name. But then I don't know that about half the fine citizens of Breen."

"Well, keep an eye on him. Let's get these horses rubbed down and square things with the livery over that one the Major borrowed. Then we'll get a drink."

"First right thing you said all night," Brody put in. Yardlinger hung back.

"What about Turk? I thought we were going to secure fresh mounts and head out to the Circle T."

"Why?" I asked. "Terwilliger's men dealt this hand."

He yanked his horse along to catch up. The piebald grunted and dug in its heels, but it was too lathered up from the hard ride to offer much resistance. "You're a peace officer! It's your job to keep the peace."

"That's only true when there's peace to keep."

Pardee was asleep in his cell when we stopped in to lock up the rifles, with one beefy arm flung across his eyes and the other flopping off the cot onto the floor. Nature carries antidotes for its own poison.

The colored livery operator gave us hell about the Major's confiscated mount, but I shut him up by giving him twice what it was worth for the time it was out and wrote out a duplicate receipt for the regular amount so his boss wouldn't know that the help was holding out on him. Yardlinger lagged behind as we approached the Glory.

"I'm not thirsty. Besides, someone's got to watch Pardee to see he doesn't hang himself."

I slid a hand under his arm. "He's too mad for that. If you don't want to drink with me, you don't have to. But I want to talk."

He looked at me with murky eyes. "I don't suppose I'll like what you have to say."

"I don't suppose so. But why start now?"

Alf, the flat-featured bartender from whom I'd taken the Schofield revolver the night before, was measuring whiskey into an ounce glass for a customer when we entered. He blanched when he saw us.

"Not again!"

I smiled and took his chin in one hand, turning his face toward the light. The mark I'd put on his cheek had turned purple and his right eye was a glistening crescent between puffed lids. "That's coming along nice. How's the gun?"

"Stinking." He pulled back out of my reach. "The action's all gummed up with sand and soap. I gave it to Thorson to clean. Meantime all I got's a busted pool cue for protection."

"Get a shotgun. I'll have some from that bottle. Major?"

"Hell, I'll have the bottle."

The saloon was filling with cattle types and girls in balding feathers and tarnished spangles, probably from Martha's. A sad-faced dandy with a burning cigarette parked behind one ear was dragging "The Ballad of Jesse James" out of the upright piano next to the stairs. Beyond him, an arch led into a smaller room in which Colleen Bower sat dealing blackjack to a gaunt redhead with tired-amused eyes, trail stubble on his chin, and a worn slouch hat on the back of his head.

"That's new." I jerked my thumb back over my shoulder as Alf pushed my drink toward me. He shrugged.

"She said she needed the money and I said all right, so long as she uses the side room. I got the Ladies' Temperance

League on my back enough as it is. Anyway, she gives the place some class."

"How much she kicking back to you?"

"House gets half."

"That isn't what I asked, Alf."

He glared at me, all wounded pride. I smiled again and flipped a coin onto the bar for the drink. It rolled, then wobbled over and buzzed to a rest.

"I'm not thinking of asking for a cut," I assured him. "I'm just curious about the going rate here."

"Two thirds," he mumbled and mopped industriously with his rag at the bar. The top was spotless to begin with.

I laughed. "You must have a thing for petticoats. In Helena they'd let her keep a dime out of every dollar. Maybe."

"This ain't Helena."

"Alf," I sighed, "I'm reminded of that every day."

"What did you want to talk about?" Having ordered a drink after all, Yardlinger leaned on one elbow so that he could view the entire room without turning. I was leaning on the opposite elbow facing him. Drinking is uncomfortable for lawmen, but not so much they give it up in droves. Major Brody placed his trust in the advertising mirror in front of him and lapped at his whiskey with both elbows on the bar.

I recounted my conversation with Dick Mather, including my convictions about Abel Turk. While I was speaking, the saddle tramp who had been playing with Colleen unfolded his long frame from the chair with a weary smile and a shake of his head and went out past us, trailing the mingled odors of horse and dust. He wore unmatched six-guns high on his narrow hips.

"You think Turk's a gunman?" Yardlinger signaled to the bartender, who poured him a second shot.

"He feels like one."

We nursed our drinks for a while in silence. Suddenly the Major snickered. "This is getting downright interesting. Chris

Shedwell coming, and a hot gun here already. Yes, sir, I'm sticking around for this one."

"If Shedwell's coming," said Yardlinger.

I said, "He's not coming. He's here."

They looked at me. I drained my glass.

"That long drink of water who walked past us a minute ago?" I prompted.

Both deputies shifted their gaze to the front door, empty now.

"Well, well," pronounced the Major, raising his glass to his lips. "Well, well."

CHAPTER 15

"Why'd you let him go?" Yardlinger's tone was accusing.

"Two reasons," I said. "First, he'll be in town for a while and we'll have plenty of other chances. Breen isn't a place you stop at on your way somewhere else. Second—"

"—You're afraid he'll kill you."

There it was, out in the open. He'd left his slouch and was standing facing me, the cloudiness gone from his eyes. I met his gaze, then caught Alf's attention and made a circular motion with my finger around the inside of my glass. He came forward to refill it.

"Not afraid. I know he'll kill me. He's dropped nine men that we know of, most of them looking at him. He's better than I am. Besides, whether you've noticed it or not, I'm not the most popular figure in this town after last night. I've heard of three men holding off a roomful of angry citizens, but the reason I've heard of it is it doesn't happen often. The next time I see Shedwell I want him alone with his back to me and a shotgun in my hands."

"Heroic."

"What do you want, a shoot-out in the street?" I was facing him again. "I call him out with my gun in its holster and my hands at my sides? Lead flying every whichway, stopping who knows where? Who told you we're supposed to be heroes?"

The piano player came to the end of his tune while I was still talking. My voice rang out across the room. Every eye in the place was on us. I tossed a silver dollar to the sad-looking musician, who caught it in one hand. "'Buffalo Gals.'"

As the music started up again, Yardlinger said: "What you're suggesting would bring you down to Shedwell's level."

"Since when was I ever above him?" I countered. "It's a game without rules and death is the only penalty. Ask the Major. How many men have you killed, Major?"

He swallowed his third drink. "Counting the war?"

"Let's say after, just to keep things manageable."

Thoughtfully he dragged his coat sleeve across his mouth. "Thirteen or fourteen. I can't be sure that redleg I gutshot in Richmond ever come around to dying. I left in kind of a hurry."

"Any of them facing you at the time?"

"Three, but two of them was unarmed and I surprised t'other. He's the one I gutshot."

"How old are you?"

"Hell, I don't know," he replied. "I never knew who my pa was, and my ma died when I was little. I raised myself. Hard on sixty, I reckon."

"You made your point." Yardlinger tossed off what was in his glass and paid for it. "I just don't happen to agree with it."

"No law against that," I said. "Just stay out of my way."

I sent him to look after our prisoner and told the Major to get some sleep. When they'd gone, I settled up with the bartender and went into the side room where Colleen Bower was playing solitaire. She had on something silver-gray with a scooping neckline that showed the line between her breasts, and her auburn hair was arranged in a pompadour with curls like sausages hanging behind her left ear. The bruise on her jaw was fading.

Three stacks of chips stood on the table next to her left elbow. At her right elbow was the handbag, open and leaning to one side from a heavy weight within.

I took the chair Shedwell had vacated and sat looking at

her. She played a card, went through the deck without success, then cleared away the layout. She didn't look up.

"You sit, you play," she said. "That's Rule Number One."

I got out the roll of bills. She shook her head.

"Rule Number Two: no cash on the table. Alf will take care of you."

I went into the main room and bought twenty dollars in chips from the bartender. Back in my seat I stacked them according to denomination and watched her shuffle the deck. I anted and she dealt us each two cards, one down, one up. I peeled up a corner of the down card, nodded. She dealt another.

"Eighteen." I turned over the five-spot.

"Twenty." She showed me a ten of hearts to go with the ten of clubs on her side and scooped up my chip along with the cards, depositing it atop one of her stacks. The cards went into deadwood, then I anted again and she dealt two more apiece. I peeped at the hole card.

"Do you know who you were playing with just now? Stand."

She took a third card, the ace of diamonds. "I know. I met him in the Cherokee Strip and again in Fort Smith. Call."

I turned up the ace of clubs. "Twenty."

"Twenty-one." She gave me a look at the four of spades and the six of diamonds and raked in the cards. Her pile grew. I anted again. She dealt.

"He say anything? Hit me."

"He said hello and that my luck had improved since Fort Smith." A card flew to each side of the table.

"I'm over." I pushed the cards away from me. They disappeared, accompanied by another chip. I lost the next two hands and said, "Let's raise the ante to five."

She shrugged and replaced the dollar chip she had in the center of the table with a five-dollar piece to match mine. I accepted two cards.

115

"Anything else?" I asked.

"You standing?"

I nodded.

"Call," she said.

"Seventeen."

"Nineteen." She turned her hole card. "Anything else such as what?" She claimed the dead cards and her booty, dealt again when I fed the pot.

"Such as, 'Your hair looks nice done like that. By the way, the Marquis de Périgueux hired me to kill Bob Terwilliger.' Or vice versa."

I lost that hand and had started to play another before she spoke again. "What he does when he's not sitting in that chair is no business of mine. Stand?"

I ignored the question, looking at her. "Withholding information from a peace officer is a misdemeanor. If he kills someone and you know about it, you'd be guilty of accessory before the fact."

Her eyes met mine. The gold flecks glittered hard as metal filings. They changed suddenly, but I was too busy playing the steel-jawed lawman to read the change. A cold snout nuzzled the nape of my neck.

"You first," said a familiar voice behind me. "Then Turk."

Both my hands were on the table. The Deane-Adams was grasped by a third and slid from its holster.

"You better move, lady. His head may not stop this bullet."

"My handbag—" she began.

"Grab it and go!" The shout stopped the piano in the main room.

She reached out as if to snatch up the bag. Her hand disappeared inside.

A bee buzzed just below my right ear and stopped with a hollow thump, simultaneous with the hoarse roar. The answering shot was so loud I didn't hear it or anything that came immediately after; it was a sudden, shocking silence that swallowed up lesser noises in a gulp. Something hot scorched the side of my head. By that time I was already in motion.

I had launched my chair over the instant her hand went into the bag. To this day I don't remember if I caught my gun as Pardee dropped it or if I scooped it up after it landed. But it was in my hand as I rolled, and with my back up against one of the table legs I felt the gun pulse and saw a black hole with a purple rim open where the foreman's left eye had been. It would have been a chest shot except that he was already sinking when it struck, his back sliding down the wall and leaving a bloody slick from the spot where Colleen's bullet had pierced the plaster after passing through his heart. His shot had been pure reflex.

He was slumped in a sitting position at the base of the wall when I scrambled to my feet, his mouth and remaining eye open and Oren Yardlinger's Navy Colt lying loose in his right hand on the floor. The room was thick with smoke. I turned to Colleen.

"Any wounds?"

"Not me." Still seated, she waved a quaking hand in the direction of the shattered plaster behind her. "I can't say the same for my handbag." She showed me the barrel of her Smith & Wesson, still smoking, protruding through a smoldering hole in the material.

Yardlinger pushed his way through the crowd gathered around the arch. He wasn't wearing his hat and his hair was in his eyes. He gaped at the corpse.

"I thought he was still asleep," he stammered. "I turned my back and he jumped me and brained me with the chamber pot. I guess he'd flattened it to get it between the bars. I woke up with my keys and my gun gone."

"Get him out of here."

He commandeered Alf and a customer and the three of them lifted the dead weight from the floor. The crowd made a path for them. Byron C. Fitch was having a big day.

Before the path could close I seized Colleen by the arm, snatched her wrap from the back of her chair, and pulled her toward the door. "Pardee has friends," I whispered, "and gunsmoke is contagious. Let's talk in my room."

She didn't resist. The clerk at the Freestone, a seedy ex-gambler in a cravat and dusty tailcoat, hardly glanced up from the desk as we passed him and continued up the stairs. I closed the door behind us and locked it.

"Every time we meet you sail a bullet past my ear." I could hardly hear myself for the whining in my skull. "Why'd you take the chance?"

She shrugged, exposing the soft valley in the U of her bodice when her wrap slipped from her shoulders. Her composure had returned. I wondered who had really killed those two half-breeds down in Yankton. "I had nothing to lose," she said. "The odds are always with the dealer." She set aside what was left of her handbag. "Is it true what you said before?"

I stared. She looked away, pretending interest in the room's furnishings.

"My hair. Do you really think it looks nice like this, or were you just being clever as usual?"

When I didn't answer she tried to outstare me, then drew the wrap tight and started past. I blocked her with my arm.

"Twenty-one." I drew her to me.

CHAPTER 16

I attended two funerals the next day, one out of respect and the other as part of my duties. I was on my way to the latter when a small man in a shabby overcoat and bucket hat approached me on the boardwalk carrying a bound stack under one arm. It was the newspaperman.

"You didn't pick these up yesterday. I don't usually deliver." He showed me a sample handbill. The legend $100 REWARD covered a third of the leaf. I gave it back.

"The situation's changed. Wait a minute." I took back the sample, got out my pencil stub, changed the hundred to a thousand and the phrase "illegal harassment of employees at the Terwilliger ranch" to "the willful murder of Dale Pardee," and returned the handbill. "Think that'll make the front page?"

He read swiftly and tucked it back under his arm. "How many columns you want?"

At the double ceremony for the Pardees the Presbyterian minister, a gaunt man with gray whiskers and salt-and-pepper hair, fixed an eagle eye on me as he said something about the wicked being given to the sword. I responded to his good wishes with a smile and a nod.

The first two pews were occupied by Circle T men in hastily brushed suits, their unruly hair slicked down with pomade and the backs of their necks pink from fresh barbering. They had filed in behind a fierce-looking old stump whose sandy hair going gray swept down past his temples from a natural break in the center when he removed his wide-brimmed hat. The pattern was repeated in a magnificent handlebar that covered all but the tip of his chin before swooping back up to underscore his jowls.

I nudged Yardlinger, who was standing beside me at the back of the room. "Terwilliger?" He nodded.

One of the hands I had seen with Pardee the night we'd met had spotted me as they'd come in and said something to the cattleman, whose faded blue eyes swung my way, nailing me to the wall before he'd continued down the aisle and taken a seat in front.

The brothers in the closed caskets before the pulpit were the only Circle T casualties. The Terwilliger men who had taken part in the raid on the Six Bar Six had lain in wait along the road and opened fire on Turk and his followers as they approached on horseback. A horse had fallen and one of Mather's men had taken a bullet in the upper arm, but they had withdrawn without additional mishap. At least that was the story told by the Mather party when they came to town to have the wound patched up.

According to Yardlinger, who had seen Pardee's companions of the previous night at the Glory, none of them were in attendance at the funeral. Mather's men were absent as well. Just in case, though, I had Major Brody stationed with a shotgun under a shaft of colored light streaming through one of the stained-glass windows. Randy Cross was at home on my orders. He was still broken up over Earl and I was afraid of what he might do in Terwilliger's presence.

The old woman who pumped the organ during the service stayed behind to prepare for Earl Trotter's send-off while we accompanied the procession to the cemetery north of town. We watched the surrounding hills for riders or the glint of sunlight on a rifle sight, and as the minister walked away from the grave dusting his palms I stepped forward to speak to Terwilliger.

I was still coming when he turned and strode toward his buggy, putting on his hat. Two Circle T men moved in to block my path. They were both armed, the horn handles of their revolvers curving over their holster tops. I backed off.

"You don't need to talk to him anyway," advised Yardlinger. "The circuit judge is due tomorrow. You can get a warrant and arrest the raiders."

"For what? Nobody saw any of their faces at the Six Bar Six. We'd just have to let them go. I was hoping to get the old man to call it square until the night riders are in custody."

An hour later we were back at the cemetery, watching Earl's remains being lowered by ropes into an open grave several yards from the fresh black soil that marked the Pardees' twin resting places. While the minister was saying his final prayers, Yardlinger pointed out a man standing where the headstone would go. Heavy-shouldered in new overalls under a shabby suit coat, he had light hair and deep lines from his reddish nose to the corners of his mouth from years of scowling. His eyes were small and shifty and he looked familiar.

"Earl's father?" I ventured.

The deputy nodded. "I'm surprised he came. With Earl's mother gone two years there was no one to drag him along."

"Probably wants to make sure he won't climb out of the box at the last minute."

Randy Cross stood at the other end of the grave with his back to us, hat in hand and head lowered. For the most part he remained still, moving only to stifle something that shuddered across his shoulders from time to time. "Are we going to be able to count on him?" I asked Yardlinger.

"Like a royal flush."

The minister tossed a handful of earth into the hole and got out of the way of the gravediggers, who picked up their spades and went to work. The bereaved father jammed a dilapidated felt hat onto his head and clumped off toward an equally hopeless wagon and team without a backward glance.

"They're burying the three dead Mather men tomorrow." The former marshal tapped a cheroot against the back of his hand, stuck it in a corner of his mouth and set fire to it. "We'll be watching that, I imagine."

I said we would. Fitch, the undertaker, had tossed the extra trade toward his rival across the street, a former partner and a slow worker. "You'd think we were running for office," I added.

"Just as well we're not. We wouldn't get many votes."

"Speaking of politics, have you heard anything from the city council?"

"Only that we seem to be holding a lot of funerals since you showed up," he said. "They don't think you're doing much for Breen's reputation."

"A lot of people would think having a bunch of night riders going around lynching people isn't good for its reputation."

"They hold you responsible for that too. If you handled things differently, maybe Fitch would be taking the day off."

I looked at him. "You agree?"

He watched the diggers, but for whom Cross was alone at the grave. "Who I agree with has nothing to do with anything. I'm just one of the Indians."

"I know you don't approve of me," I said. "All I ask is that you stick around and see this through. Then you can do whatever you want."

"Last night you told me to stay out of your way."

"I was tired and not in a very good mood. I can use you. Cross too. Even the Major."

As if he had heard his name, the old rebel approached us wobbling on his bowed legs. "This here was a good'un," he announced. "Hell of a lot better'n that one they give the Pardees. I like that part about dust and ashes. Bet I heard it a million times and I still can't get enough of it. Bet you're the same way." He winked at me.

"The Major likes funerals," Yardlinger explained.

"So I noticed. Find out yet where Shedwell's staying?"

"I asked," nodded the chief deputy. "The Breen House, Room sixteen."

I chewed my lip. "He must be in the gold."

"Or expecting to be," he finished.

"Get Cross."

In the office twenty minutes later, I handed around the shotguns, keeping one of the 10-gauge Remingtons for myself. "Does the Breen House have a back door?"

Yardlinger laughed shortly.

"A hotel with a back door? They might as well give the rooms away free."

"Good. You and Randy stay out front and keep an eye on the entrance. Major, I want you watching the windows behind the building. If Shedwell comes out, kill him."

"Just like that?" bristled Yardlinger. "No provocation?"

I stared him down. "If he comes out alone, it means I'm dead. Is that provocation enough?"

"Hell, yes," Brody croaked. "You ain't even in season."

The prissy clerk backed away from the desk as I came through the door. "Afternoon," I said, leaning my palms on top of the desk. "Is Chris Shedwell in?"

"There's no one registered by that name," he replied stiffly.

"You get a lot of transients. How do you know that without looking at the book?" I leaned closer. "We could push this back and forth for an hour: You open the book to prove he isn't registered, I describe him, you say, 'Oh, yes, that's Mr. Dollarsworth, the cattle buyer from Chicago,' I ask you again if he's in, you tell me you're not at liberty to say, I grab you by the hair and shove my gun barrel down your throat. But I don't have that much time and you don't have the teeth to spare. So why don't you save us both the trouble and tell me if he's in his room."

123

His waxed moustache had lost its curl while I was talking. "Room sixteen, top floor."

"I know that. Do you expect him down soon?"

"I couldn't say." Hastily he added, "He hasn't been down for lunch."

"Fine. I'll wait."

I took a seat inside the curl of the staircase on a settee upholstered in green chintz that reminded me of the furniture at Martha's, the shotgun across my knees. Thoughts of Martha brought me around to Colleen, but I quickly put her out of my head. I'd once asked an old wolfer the secret behind his impressive kill record and he'd said, "I just think wolf." I was thinking Shedwell.

I'd been sitting there ten minutes by the standing clock beside the front desk when the stairs above me started creaking. I got up quietly and shifted the shotgun to ready.

The noise grew louder, and then a pair of boots came into view at about eye level on the carpeted steps. I forced my fingers to relax on the Remington's stock. I was on the blind side of anyone coming downstairs.

In another moment he had reached the floor and crossed to the desk, a pudgy drummer type in a knee-length overcoat and a derby cocked at a jaunty angle. He was carrying a carpetbag in one hand and a piece of paper in the other. I sank back against the wall.

He glanced around the lobby without seeing me, stopped at the desk, and showed the paper to the clerk, who studied it and pointed at me. The drummer turned and came toward me. He wore a thin moustache and an embarrassed smile. I leveled the shotgun at his belt buckle. He stopped ten feet away. He was no longer smiling.

"Who are you?" I demanded.

His mouth worked a little before he got it out. "Carpenter."

"You don't look like one. What's in there, your tools?"

He glanced down at his bag, as if expecting to see saws and

hammers poking out. "No, no," he stammered. "Carpenter's my name. Felix Carpenter. I sell harnesses. The gentleman upstairs asked me to give this to the man in the lobby." He held up the scrap of paper. It rattled in his hand.

"What gentleman?"

"Tall, thin fellow. Red hair." The noise the paper was making almost drowned out his words.

"Put it on the floor and get out."

He bent and placed it on the carpet, then backed away.

"Hey!" cried the clerk. "What about the bill?"

Felix Carpenter fingered a wallet out of his coat and flung a handful of bills onto the desk. The clerk was still counting them when the door closed on his late guest.

Crabwalking to keep an eye on the staircase, I went over and picked up the square of paper. It was hotel stationery. The message was printed unevenly in ink under the name of the establishment.

Dear Marshal,

Cold in the lobby aint it how about coming up for a drink your friends are welcome too.

Shedwell

CHAPTER 17

The door to Room 16 was partially open when I reached the fourth floor, light spilling across the leaf-patterned hall runner. I stopped a few doors away, wondering if I should have taken Shedwell at his word and brought along the deputies. But I didn't want too many guns going off in cramped quarters if it came to that.

I considered the options, his as well as mine. In his place I might have left the door open as bait and crouched inside a vacant room nearby until someone like me walked past. Then I would have stepped out and emptied my cylinder at his back. Shotgun leveled, I rattled every doorknob between the staircase and 16, alternating between opposite sides of the hallway. All were locked.

There were three ways I could go from there. I could hit the floor as I entered, as I had done at the Freestone when the two ranchers were waiting for me in my room, and hope that any lead that flew would be directed at a standing target, or I could wait for him to make the first move, as I had done a long time ago waiting for a killer at that cabin in Missoula. Or I could walk in bold as brass and give him a clear chance at me.

To hell with it. I'd been brained, drawn on, shot at, and ambushed and I was tired of being careful. I filled my lungs and stepped inside.

Right away I knew I'd made a mistake.

It was a room like Marshal Arno's, richly carpeted and

furnished. A trail-battered valise with a rolled-leather handle worn fuzzy sat on the floor next to the too-high bed. A slouch hat I recognized occupied the mattress. No Shedwell.

A voice inside me shouted, *Get away from the door*. But before I could move there was a snick of metal across the hall, two quick footsteps on the runner, and death in a steel case punched my right kidney.

"Move and you're wainscoting."

Then again, if I were in Shedwell's position, I might have figured that my stalker was smart enough to try all the doors and would have locked the one to my hiding place and risked the delay.

The voice at my ear was soft, barely more than a whisper, and carried a lilting accent I couldn't identify from those few words. A hand protruding from a blue-flannel sleeve curled around in front of me and relieved me of the shotgun. The hand was freckled, with fine red hairs curling on the back. I started to raise my hands but stopped when the gun prodded me again.

"Fold your arms across your chest. That's the boy."

While my revolver was being taken from its holster I concentrated on the accent. Irish. The hand reappeared to pat my chest, slide under both arms, press the side pockets of my jacket, and feel my legs down to my boots. He took his time and made a thorough job of it. Clothing rustled as he straightened.

"Don't turn around yet. Go over to the bed and sit down."

I did as directed, perching on the edge of the mattress. This put him within my field of vision. He closed the door without turning and stood to one side of it, a tall man as lean as Yardlinger but not as tense, with an open face dusted with freckles, blue eyes, and rust-colored hair beginning to recede at the temples. Sunburned skin formed scales on his nose and at the tops of his cheeks. He had shaved since last night and he was smiling broadly.

"You'd be Page Murdock. I can tell by the gun." He had holstered his own revolver and was examining the Deane-Adams. The shotgun was leaning in the corner next to the door.

I didn't bother to acknowledge my identity. "You must have seen us coming through the window. I thought of that, but I couldn't see any way around it."

He shrugged. He wore a sheepskin vest over his blue shirt, mottled jeans stuffed into the tops of dusty brown boots cracking at the arches. His gun belt was strapped high, the butts positioned for easy grasping as he brought his hands up from his thighs. The revolver in his right holster was a Remington Frontier .44 with a smooth white grip. Its mate was lighter, constructed along the lines of the Deane-Adams, and its grip was hickory or walnut. I read an article once that said he carried twenty-three notches, but if he did, it wasn't evident during his stay in Breen. I broke the silence.

"Is that a Starr forty-four in your left holster?"

He nodded. "But I don't use it as a double-action. I cock it every time, else I might get confused betwixt it and the Remington."

"The caps jam the action anyway when you don't cock it," I added. "What about the Remington? I'm told it's barrel-heavy."

"I like them that way. Keeps my hand steady."

A china clock ticked away on the fireplace mantel. Two businessmen whiling away the afternoon talking shop. "Shoot with either hand?" I asked.

"Border shift. I collected some lead in my left elbow down in Lincoln County. These days it's not much good above the waist."

I grunted. "I'm supposed to believe that?"

He smiled again and said nothing. He looked more like an Irish rebel than a western gunman. The writers who were busy shaping his legend couldn't decide whether he was born in New York City or Boston, but his speech and appearance placed him closer to County Cork.

He played with the English revolver, turning the cylinder and taking it on and off cock. "We almost met when I was marshal in Wichita. Did you know that?"

"Enough to make sure we didn't," I replied.

"They told me you was in town shipping cattle with the Harper outfit. You had kind of a reputation then. There was some wanted me to give you a try. I said I reckon not."

"They were saying the same thing on my side. I keep reading about famous triggers shooting it out, but I've never heard of it really happening."

"That's because you don't make a reputation dying young."

He was having fun and we both knew it. Face to face with Chris Shedwell I didn't stand a chance. I said, "Well, that was a long time ago, and now the boot's in the other stirrup."

"I heard you was looking for me. What you doing here anyway? Talk is you're wearing tin for R. B. Hayes."

"I am. The job here is just a hobby to keep me busy during my vacation."

His face looked grim for the first time since we'd been talking. "It's that mail train thing, ain't it?"

"They say you killed the clerk in the express car near Wichita just to get back at the city council for dismissing you as marshal," I said.

"That's stupid. If I wanted to do something like that, it'd be one of the ones fired me I'd kill. Besides, I wasn't dismissed. I had a contract with the council and it run out. Am I the reason you're in town?"

"One of them."

"The main one, I'll warrant. Well, I hope you didn't waste too much public money getting here. Was I a taxpayer I'd write my congressman and complain, if I had a congressman." He set aside my gun and dug a travel-worn fold of paper out of his breast pocket.

I got up carefully and reached to pluck the scrap from his outstretched hand. If civilization was measured by the amount of paper that changed possession in the space of a few days, civilization had come to Breen.

It was a document signed by the sheriff of Sedgwick County, Kansas, and bearing the seal of a notary public, to the effect that Christopher Sarsfield Shedwell had been cleared of all charges connected with the robbery of the mail car on the Union Pacific Railroad and the shooting death of postal clerk Aloysius Garvey on September 4, 1877. It was dated last May 22. I read it twice, refolded it, and put it in a pocket.

"I'll have to confirm it with the Sedgwick County sheriff."

"Figured you would. I'd like that back after. I've had to show it to every lawman betwixt here and Fargo."

"Why didn't you say something before?"

He studied me with eyes the color of lake water when you break through the ice on a clear winter morning.

"Couple of years back I killed a Pinkerton in a fair fight in a town I don't recollect the name of in Idaho and took to the mountains. That was dead December, and the wind was like razors. I lived in a shallow cave for eleven days, eating sardines cold with my fingers and potting at Pinkertons' heads whenever they showed themselves until they gave up and went back to town. I was found innocent at the inquest, but I still have to cross the street every time I spot a Pinkerton or shoot it out."

"Is there a point to that story?" I asked, when he didn't go on.

"Only that after a man's got through something like that, he don't place a lot of trust in a piece of paper to pry him out of a tight spot."

"If this is confirmed, I'll wire Judge Blackthorne. In a month every jailhouse west of the Alleghenies will have a copy."

"That's if I let you leave here," he said.

I paused. "What's the percentage in killing me?"

"Them writers back East could do a lot with me outshooting Page Murdock."

"Not much. I'm not well known, thank God. I've got better things to do with my time than spend half of it practicing my fast draw and the other half taking on all comers. And I try to avoid mountains in the wintertime."

"I got all the reputation I need anyway." He extended the Deane-Adams, butt first. I was reaching for it when he spun it and I found myself looking down the bore.

"Wes Hardin pulled that one on Hickok in Abilene a few years back," I said. "You're stealing material."

"Who do you think taught it to me?" He handed me the revolver and then the shotgun. "We'll meet again, most likely, but that time the rules will be different."

I put the gun away. "Don't give me rules. You're not talking to one of those eastern writers. Who paid your way to Breen?"

Creases in his face made him not much younger than I, but when he smiled they vanished, the years falling from him like dead bark from a log. "Sure, rules," he said. "I'm supposed to keep why I'm here a secret and you're supposed to find out." He opened the door and held it for me.

He followed me down to the second-floor landing, where he hung back. I felt his eyes on me all the way across the lobby and out the front door.

CHAPTER 18

"What is this, the honor system?" Yardlinger sneered. He and Randy Cross were standing on the boardwalk on either side of the hotel entrance, holding their shotguns. "You go on to the jail and wait for Shedwell to turn himself in?"

"I'll explain later. Get the Major." I turned and stepped back inside, leaving them there.

The clerk raised his eyebrows at my return. "Step around in front," I commanded. "Come on, come on. I promise not to shoot you."

Reluctantly he obeyed, cringing slightly as if he'd left his pants behind. Keeping one eye on the staircase landing, now deserted, I stood next to him and measured. I had maybe half an inch on him. Close enough.

"Take off your coat."

He stared, opened his mouth to speak, then drew it shut. Awkwardly he peeled off his black swallowtail. His shoulders came off with it. I shrugged out of my own canvas jacket and told him to put it on. He hesitated, then complied, draping his coat over the desk. He looked like a scarecrow in his new attire, but from a distance he could pass. I took off my hat and put it on his head. It went right past his ears and settled on the bridge of his long nose. I lifted it from him, glanced around, then, ignoring his protests, tore two blank pages from the open register and stuffed them into the sweatband. That made it a perfect fit.

"You'll find three men waiting out front," I said. "You know them, they're my deputies. Go with them to the marshal's office and wait there for me. Tell them I told you to do that."

"The desk," he explained. "Someone has to watch it."

I had him by the shoulders and was pushing him toward the door. "It'll still be here when you get back. Didn't you ever play lawman when you were a boy? Here's your chance to relive your childhood."

"My mother wouldn't let me play. I had to stay inside and practice the vio—" The door slammed on the rest of it.

Striding back across the lobby, I shoved the clerk's coat down behind the desk out of sight and took up my original station inside the staircase curve. I considered the logistics, then lay the shotgun across the chintz-covered settee. In close quarters a long gun can be worse than no weapon at all. Then I waited.

I had time enough to hope that the deputies would take the clerk at his word and accompany him to the office rather than enter the lobby to confirm what he told them, and then there were footsteps on the stairs and Chris Shedwell's dusty brown boots appeared coming down. I stepped back farther into the curve.

The Deane-Adams was slippery in my grasp. I changed hands and wiped my palm on my shirt. Then I switched back, willing myself to relax once again until the revolver snuggled easily into my grip. I had done all this hundreds of times before and didn't have to think about it any more than a woodchopper has to concentrate before spitting on his hands and taking hold of the axe.

He hit the carpeted floor at an easy lope, swiveling his head left and right out of old habit to take in the entire lobby. My nook protected me from observation. He was wearing his hat and a Confederate officer's gray coat with captain's epaulets and powder burns around a patch on the left elbow. He'd ridden guerrilla during the war and I wondered if he'd been wounded in the fighting or if he had told the truth about getting shot in Lincoln County. Or if the coat had come from a dead man.

A third of the way across the room he stopped. The unoccupied desk had alerted him. He grasped his Remington and started to turn. The sound of the Deane-Adams' hammer was like dried acorns crunching in the empty lobby. He froze.

"What you said before about wainscoting?" I reminded him.

He held that position for a beat, and then he slowly raised both hands and started to fold them across his chest. I told him to keep raising them. I didn't know but that he was wearing a third weapon in a shoulder sling.

"Turn around."

He did so, looking amused as far up as his freckled and peeling cheeks. You wouldn't have known it from his eyes.

"The clerk," he said. "I should have figured that wasn't you crossing the street. I used that trick ducking vigilantes in Denver."

"Who do you think taught it to me?"

"Dime novels." He grinned. "Them writers'll kill us all yet."

"And write about it afterwards. Who hired you, Périgueux, Mather, or Terwilliger? Or was it someone else?"

"Don't know the gentlemen. I'm here on a social visit."

"Colleen Bower?"

His eyes widened slightly, then returned to normal. "They said you was fast. I thought they meant guns."

"Breen's the north side of hell. You didn't ride all this way just to see a woman."

"She's got a fine Irish name." He leaned on the brogue. "Maybe I'm homesick."

"Annie isn't an Irish name, and we don't know that that's hers either."

"You don't know mine's Shedwell."

135

"I think it is. No one would call himself Sarsfield if he had a choice. You're running out of answers."

"But you won't shoot," he said. "On account of I ain't here to sell my gun and that paper in your pocket says I ain't wanted. So what say we get us some supper? I been sleeping almost since I got in. I ain't ate at table going on three weeks."

"No one knows I have that paper but you and me. As far as anyone out here is concerned, you're fair game."

He mulled that over. Then he shook his head. "If you was thinking that way, you'd of put one through me before this."

"I never could bluff," I sighed, letting down the hammer. "Eat your supper and clear out. Just remember that the next time a cowboy dies within a day's ride of town you won't survive him by long."

"I don't intend to."

He wasn't smiling as he said it, and I was still thinking about it after he had gone through the door that led into the hotel restaurant.

I went back to the office to put away the shotgun and trade coats with the clerk, who on his way out muttered something about the wisdom of staying in Chicago. Cross and the Major had gone home. Yardlinger watched me from behind the desk. He was still wearing his hat, something he rarely did indoors.

"I guess I'll have to wait for your autobiography to find out what all that was about," he said.

I dropped into one of the other chairs, suddenly weary. "It won't take up much space. See what you think of that." I flipped the folded document Shedwell had given me onto the desk. He read it swiftly, then looked up.

"Think it's genuine?"

"What am I, a forgery expert? Wire Sedgwick County. If he's like any other lawman the sheriff will be eating supper about now. Tell them to send the reply here and get something to eat meanwhile."

He got up and stretched, bones cracking. "Want something sent over?"

"I lost my appetite at the hotel." I tilted my hat forward.

I must have dozed, because when I opened my eyes again it was dark out. I turned up the lamp just as Colleen Bower walked in. She was wearing something that caught the light and threw it back, and clutching her wrap at the neck. Her cheeks were rosy from the cold, or maybe it was rouge.

"Someone steal your handbag?" I asked. "It can't be worth much with that hole you blew in it."

She stopped halfway between the door and the desk. "You're drunk."

"I'd like to be, but I'm just tired." Then I read her expression. "What is it?"

"Dick Mather's hands are going to hit Terwilliger's Circle T tomorrow morning."

I started to rise, then sat back down. Playing it close to the vest. "How do you know?"

"Some men from the Six Bar Six are at Martha's. I overheard them discussing it in the parlor. They're drunk and loud."

"Sure?"

She tilted her chin. "That they're drunk or that I overheard them?"

"That they're making plans. Never mind." I remembered that I was still wearing my hat and took it off, placing it on the desk. Mother would have approved. "Why come to me?"

"I thought you might be interested." Her tone dripped ice.

"I mean, why should you care? You'll excuse me if I look this particular gift horse in the mouth, but what good is even a free mount with bad teeth?"

"Don't you trust me by now?"

"If you're talking about last night, that doesn't have much to do with anything."

"Miss Jessup was right. She told us that men lose their respect for women who say yes." She started to turn away, then stopped. "Maybe I wanted to make your job a little easier. Maybe I think there's been enough murder done in this vicinity."

I waited, but she didn't say anything more. "What time tomorrow morning?"

"First light."

"Thanks. Anything else?"

Her lips parted, then pressed together, etching unbecoming lines from mouth to nostrils. She drew the wrap tighter about her shoulders, spun, and flounced out, her heels knocking the boardwalk until the noise was lost in the waning traffic outside.

Minutes later a boy entered with my answer from Wichita. I paused in the midst of checking the loads in the long guns to tip him and open the envelope. A cowhand convicted of the strangling death of his common-law wife north of Hays had confessed to the lone robbery of the mail train the night before his hanging, lifting suspicion from Chris Shedwell.

"I'll be damned."

"Is that your answer, Marshal?"

I'd forgotten the messenger was still there. I shook my head and sent him off. Yardlinger returned as I was locking up the guns. I showed him the wire and briefed him on what Colleen had told me. Sitting in the customer's chair, he played with a pen and listened in silence until I finished.

"You believe her?" he asked then.

"I was going to ask you the same question. You've known her longer than I have."

"But not as well."

I grinned. "For some reason, given my obvious appeal, I've never been able to convince myself that I'm the Lord's gift to womankind. When one of them starts confiding secrets I always feel for my poke."

He tested the pen's nib on the ball of his thumb. "There's another explanation. Remember what I said about the second rule of successful gambling."

"If she wants to stay on the right side of the law, she wouldn't dangle false bait," I agreed.

"And she did save your hide last night."

"Hers too, don't forget. You never know where a bullet's going to land in a small room. Besides, leading us into an ambush would improve her standing with the cattlemen on both sides. They'd be calling the shots once we're dead."

"Sounds like you've talked yourself into disbelieving her story." He stopped playing with the pen.

I shook my head. "I've talked myself around in a full circle. One thing's sure, though. We can't ignore it."

He pushed himself out of his chair, flipping the pen so that it stuck in the stained blotter for a moment before flopping over. "I'll get Randy and the Major."

"No hurry. Just say what's on the fire and tell them to meet us here at three o'clock. We'll need all the sleep we can buy between now and then." I stood and put on my hat. "I've got some doors to try before I turn in."

"Think you should?"

"If I don't, Mather's men will suspect something. Besides, ducking lead is one of my many talents."

With darkness, the action in town had moved indoors, leaving the streets deserted but for the occasional transient making his unsteady way between saloons. A shoe-heel moon shed milkwater light over the east side of the street. I confined the early patrol to the facing side, where the shadows lay. That's one thing you gave up when you accepted a star, the right to walk in the light. City marshals were targets at the best of times, but in a wide-open town they were always in season.

I'd kept to the shadows so long that I was beginning to grow leather wings and sleep upside down.

Piano music spilled out of the saloons as I walked past, snatches of tunes mingling with the general racket of loud talk and drunken laughter, now riding a wave of warm air tainted with stale smoke and old beer, now fading to a whimper as I left the barrooms behind to rattle the doorknobs of darkened shops and peer through shuttered windows. I took my time crossing alleys, where a tongue of blue flame licking from the darkness could send me rolling for my life in the dust or kneeling in my own blood, depending on whether I detected anything before the trigger was squeezed. But they were quiet.

I was on my way back across the street when Yardlinger emerged from the Pick Handle with Major Brody in tow. We met just off the boardwalk.

"Randy's inside," reported the chief deputy. "Dead drunk."

I cursed. "He picked a fine time for it."

"He's still busted up over Earl. We can't talk to him."

"Think we should start pouring coffee and salt into him, Cap'n?" Brody asked.

"That depends on whether he's a mean drunk."

He grinned toothlessly. "There's other kinds?"

"Then let him go till he fags out. We'll have enough people trying to kill us in the morning without starting early." I gave Yardlinger what was left of the roll I'd brought from Helena. "Hand that to the bartender and tell him if Randy isn't in a bed—any bed—by midnight I'll close him down permanently."

"Honey and vinegar in one dish. You don't take chances." He went back into the saloon.

Alone with me, the Major sawed an inch off his tobacco plug and popped it into his mouth. "Shooting tomorrow, I hear."

I confirmed it with a nod. Coal-oil light from the saloon clung to us dirty and yellow.

"I do believe for the first time in my life I've had enough already."

I studied him. "That mean you want out?"

"Didn't say that." There was a twinkle in his eye that, had I still money, I'd have bet was the last thing a lot of men had seen this side of Gabriel's horn.

I was still watching him when the shooting started.

CHAPTER 19

I didn't hear the hoofbeats until they were right on top of us. Later I found out they'd stopped before the city limits and bound the horses' feet with gunny sacks to muffle the noise. At the time, all I heard was a strange thumping behind me and turned just as a demon bore down on me, riding a black horse with red fire at its eyes and nostrils and swinging a cavalry saber that snatched the light as it came around and swept my hat off my head. If I hadn't ducked at the flash, my head would have come off with it. Then the horse was pounding past, sideswiping me and knocking me staggering. But I caught a glimpse of the rider's face, or lack of it, dead white with black holes for eyes.

The street was alive with them, hollow-eyed and faceless astride coal-black horses, their muffled hoofbeats sounding like rapid shots miles away. Only these sounds were right here and I was in the midst of them. Sabers whistled. Once I heard a noise like a cook's cleaver striking half-boiled meat, a nauseating sound. Then there were real shots, hard and sharp, like derisive coughs, and metal-gray smoke that mingled with the white vapor exhaled by the horses.

The rider who had swiped at me spun his horse and came back for a second try. I tore out the Deane-Adams and snapped off a quick shot, not hoping to hit him, just teach him some respect. Lead was singing all around me. I didn't wait to see if my bullet had any effect, but dived between the horizontal logs that supported the boardwalk and scrambled around until I was facing out, my cheek resting on the hand holding the gun.

There might have been twelve riders. There might have been a hundred. With their frantic galloping this way and that and the layer of black-powder smoke that hung in the still air, there was no way of counting them. The boards above me creaked and I heard a hammering above those and knew that Yardlinger had left the saloon to make use of his Navy Colt. A deeper roar announced the arrival of Cross's shotgun. Another revolver joined in, probably the Major's. I fired at a white head, but then it was lost in the confusion and smoke and I didn't know if I'd hit anything.

Presently a horse went down whinnying, rolled completely over, and struggled to its feet, favoring its shattered left rear leg and leaving its rider spread-eagled in the dust, his pale oversize head bobbing like an India rubber balloon on a string. Hoarse screams wound their way through the popping pistols and thudding hoofs. Then they stopped altogether. The galloping and shooting continued, around and around, this way and that, as if a gang of children had been turned loose in a fenced-in playground.

Something landed on the boards overhead like a sack of grain and an arm flopped in front of my face. It wore a black coat sleeve. The hand uncurled and Oren Yardlinger's Navy Colt swung loose from the trigger guard hooked on his index finger.

Bitter rage swept through me. Working mostly by feel, I thumbed out my spent cartridges, replaced them, and squeezed the trigger again and again, moving my arm in a wide arc along the ground from left to right and back, the gun throbbing in my grasp. I felt its kick, saw the smoke whooshing out the barrel and through the space between the cylinder and the frame, but I was too intent on my fleeting targets to hear my own reports. I heard glass shattering on the other side of the street and knew that I was responsible for some of

144

it. Whether or not I was hitting anything in between made little difference in the general uproar. Horses turned and galloped and shook their manes and reared to paw the air with their sack-clad hoofs, blue and orange spurts lashing across their necks and over their heads behind a motionless veil of smoke, like something going on outside a clouded window. And then they were gone.

As quickly as that. One moment the street was alive with men and horses and the next only the smoke remained, drifting cautiously now as if unsure that it was safe to depart. Silence crackled.

I kept cover for what felt like an hour. Then impatience overcame caution and I wriggled out of my hiding place inches at a time, ready to scramble back under at the first shot. None came. I was alone on the street, or so I thought.

I stood, brushing unconsciously at the dust and dried manure on my front. The opposite side of the street was even darker now, with blank spots where before there had been window panes to throw back the light from this side. The air was raw gunsmoke. Somewhere in the shadows a sheet of glass the size of a dinner plate dropped loose and struck a sill, parting with a clank. I whirled and squeezed off in that direction from reflex. The hammer snapped on an empty shell.

On both sides it seemed there was scarcely a building whose woodwork wasn't bullet-chewed and whose windows didn't sport missing panes and dollar-size holes. A sign that had swung from chains under the porch roof of the harness shop swayed dangling at the end of a single set of links, its legend shot away and the broken chain trailing like a kite tail. Even the hitching rail on this side looked worm-eaten, though minutes before its new wood had stood out nakedly against the weathered planking behind it. The next day's edition of the Breen *Democrat* would report that more than one hundred and fifty shots had been fired within six minutes, and I would wonder if the editor had crouched behind one of his typecases tallying them on a pad.

Most of the lamps in the business section were out, either destroyed by bullets or turned out when the shooting started. Yellow light flared and faltered in one of the saloons, where an aproned bartender and one or two volunteers labored with wet towels and slop buckets to put out a fire probably started when a lamp broke.

The rider I had seen go down under his horse lay still in the street with arms and legs spread like spokes in a wheel, crushed into the two-inch deep dust and resembling a pasteboard doll discarded and forgotten. He wore a pillowcase over his head with circles cut out for his eyes, which accounted for the swollen white heads I had been shooting at. It was tucked into his collar and tied down with a cord. I stepped over and tore it off.

He was young, hardly more than twenty if he was that. His moustache and side-whiskers barely covered the flesh beneath. A soft moist glaze coated his eyes and his mouth was frozen open. I had never seen him before.

A whistling snort brought my attention to a lone black horse standing near the livery, where it had undoubtedly been drawn by the familiar smells of manure and feed. It was strapped into a scaled-down saddle like cowboys used and held its left rear leg aloft at an unnatural angle. I had seen it fall when that leg shattered and I was standing over the man who had fallen with it.

Sighing, I reloaded the Deane-Adams and took aim at the animal's head. Page Murdock, the Fearless Horse-Slayer of the Plains. Before I could fire there was a hard, flat bang and the black folded down onto its right side with a grunting sigh.

I pulled down on the bullet's source and held back at the last instant. Major Brody came rocking toward me, trailing smoke from his big Peacemaker. He was as dirty as I was in front, having just crawled from under a buckboard next to the dry goods emporium. His left shoulder was smeared with something darker than the dust on the street.

"That's twice someone's claimed a target of mine since I got here," I complained. My voice sounded strange in the silence following the final shot. I put away the gun, nodding toward his stained shoulder. "Bad?"

He shook his head. His face was black with powder. I supposed mine was too. "Bastard glanced a saber off'n it. I shot him in the guts, though. He won't get far."

I remembered the noise of a cleaver striking meat. "Let's have a look at it."

"We'll tend to Oren first."

I realized with a pang of guilt that I hadn't thought about the chief deputy since his arm had dropped in front of me. Yardlinger was lying on his face with one boot hooked inside the threshold of the Pick Handle, his hat bunched forward and the hand holding the gun still hanging over the edge of the boardwalk. We turned him over as gently as possible, considering his one hundred and seventy pounds of muscle, and laid him on his back. The right side of his face was covered with blood and I thought at first that half his head was gone. Then he groaned.

"Water!" I barked. The Major ducked into the saloon, to reappear moments later carrying a full bucket. When he set it down I soaked my kerchief in it, wrung it out, and, supporting the wounded man's head with my free hand, used the makeshift washrag to clean off the blood.

A bullet had carried away part of his eyebrow, leaving a two-inch long furrow along his temple. As I dabbed at the congealing leakage, his eyes fluttered open and he tried to speak.

I said, "Don't bother explaining. Anyone who stands up in the middle of all that flying lead deserves to lose a lot more than his good looks. Is he hit anywhere else?" This to Brody.

He searched Yardlinger for blood spots, loosened a button here and there and then did it up. He shook his head.

"Fetch the doctor," I said.

"No need."

The speaker was built small, with thin wrists protruding like brittle sticks from too-short coat sleeves, no cuffs, and carrying a black leather bag that looked new. He wore a sandy moustache and looked about fifteen but for that. "Orville Ballard," he introduced himself.

I stared at him. "Discovered girls yet?"

"What did you expect?" he snarled. "An old, established practitioner? They don't come out here. Only drunks, charlatans, and untried medical school graduates."

"Which are you?"

He smiled thinly behind the moustache. He was down on one knee already and rummaging through his bag. "You got lucky. I hate alcohol and when I lie my ears get red."

I watched suspiciously as he examined the wound. Then he lit a match and pulled open each of the wounded man's eyes to study them in the flickering light. That done, he unstoppered a small bottle of peroxide, inserted a cotton swab, and applied the strong-smelling stuff to the gash along Yardlinger's temple. The patient flinched and said something about the doctor's ancestry.

At that point I relaxed, rocking back on my heels. Out there you were grateful when what passed for the local physician didn't strap feathers around his head and cut a chicken into pieces to read the entrails.

"Where's Randy?" I asked the Major.

He was holding his injured shoulder, fresh blood seeping between his fingers. His head tilted toward the saloon. "Warming a chair with his shotgun on his knees. Fagged out."

I got up and took a step toward the door. There was a deep bellow and six inches of door casing disintegrated next to my head. I ducked.

"Reckon he woke up," Brody suggested.

I raised my voice. "Randy, it's me, Murdock. If you do that again I'll ram that shotgun down your throat. Sideways."

There was a silence, then: "C'mon in, Page. Damn. I thought you was one of them bushwhackers come for another go." He slurred his consonants.

I started forward again, then twisted around and picked up the bucket of water the Major had brought from the saloon. To the doctor I said, "When you're through with Yardlinger, take a look at the old man's arm."

The moonlit barroom was a shambles of overturned tables and broken glass. I crunched through it to where Cross was slouched in a chair, hat pushed far back on his head, and the short scattergun in his lap. The back door stood open, marking the path of the other occupants' retreat at the height of the melee.

"You all in one piece?" I asked Cross.

His teeth gleamed in a slow, lopsided grin. "Hell, yes," he drawled, and belched. "Why shouldn't I be?"

"Good." I swung the full bucket back in both hands and dashed its contents into his face. It struck with a noise like wet rags slapping a fence, drenching him from crown to sole. He coughed and sputtered and pawed his face with his big hands.

His mouth was working like a fish's, but before he could say anything I hurled the bucket away and said, "Climb into something dry and ride out to the Circle T. Tell Terwilliger if he wants the men who lynched his foreman's brother to arm his hands and send them to town. There's a tracking moon and I need special deputies. Get going!"

I shouted the last two words. Galvanized, Cross sprang from his seat and lurched dripping toward the door, considerably more sober than he had been moments before. I followed him out.

Yardlinger was sitting up with his back against a porch

post, a white bandage holding a patch of gauze to his injury. In shirtsleeves now, the doctor was kneeling over Major Brody, lying coatless on his back with his head resting on the physician's folded garment. Someone had provided a lantern that shed cheery light from a nail on the post. A lot of blood stained the planks around the old man, too much.

"Why didn't you have me look at him first?" spat the doctor as I emerged from the Pick Handle. "His arm almost came off with his coat!"

I squatted next to the Major, whose blackened face glistened in the lantern light. "You told me the saber glanced off."

He grinned without teeth. It might have been a wince.

"It must of." His voice was a harsh whisper. "Else the arm would of dropped off right then."

I smiled in spite of myself. One-armed he'd have taken on all hell's host if he smelled a ruckus in it.

"Now's as good a time to tell you as any," he said then. "Day you taken over you said something about a deputy selling information to the Frenchie."

"I knew it was you the minute we met," I put in.

He looked puzzled. Then his face twisted into a mask of agony. Ballard was using a short pair of scissors to cut his shirtsleeve away from the wound.

"It stood to reason," I went on. "Périgueux could afford to pay a stiff price for intelligence. Randy was too loyal and Earl was too stupid. You were the only one left."

I had to bend closer to hear what he said next. "It was just that one time. I only done it 'cause I was bored. I ain't been bored since you come."

"Forget it. You did a damn fine job tonight. Without that Peacemaker we'd still be dodging lead."

The bewildered look returned. "Hell, I was reloading when they decided to chuck it. I thought it was you."

I let my hands dangle between my knees. "That doesn't

make any sense. I was banging away like an idiot under the boardwalk. Yardlinger was down and Cross only fired one barrel. I . . ."

My silence alerted the doctor, busy trying to staunch the flow of blood from Brody's mangled shoulder. He glanced up at me, then followed my gaze. Chris Shedwell was crossing the street in our direction.

CHAPTER 20

His face meant nothing to the doctor, who resumed his labors at the Major's side. I stepped off the boardwalk to meet the mankiller. He was wearing his Confederate coat.

"Why?" I asked. "Or don't you shed enough blood in your work?"

His eyebrows went up a quarter inch. He had an expressive face, not at all the kind you'd expect a professional gunman to possess. "I figured gratitude was too much to hope for," he said. "I didn't expect to be called out, though. Next time I'll maybe mind my own business."

"I wish I knew what your business was."

He favored me with the famous Shedwell smile. "Don't jump to conclusions. The fact is I decided to make an early night and I got sort of smoked with all that noise under my window. Thought I'd pick off an ear or two just to spread some education."

I watched him. I've said he didn't have a poker face, but his expressions didn't necessarily match his meaning. "Well, thanks for the help. You wouldn't care to carry the lesson out of town?"

"That'd be vindictive," he said. "I mean, just over a few minutes' sleep lost."

"Suit yourself." I left him, approaching the fallen horse. Its eyes were frozen with the whites showing and its tongue was dusty between its teeth. The saddle blanket covered the flank. I flipped it up to get a look at the brand. A vertical bar with a

153

numeral 6 burned on either side—Mather's Six Bar Six. What else? I spotted the Negro who ran the livery standing among the spectators nearby and called him over.

"Yess'r?" His face was like dull, crumpled foil under a floppy hat and he was wearing three shirts over dingy flannels, the tails hanging outside his gray, shapeless trousers.

I nudged the dead horse with the toe of my boot. "Drag this carcass into the stable and hold it till someone comes for it. It's evidence in an assault case and possibly a lynching."

"I gots to talk to the boss," he said, rubbing his chin with a big horny hand. "We ain' never kep' no dead aminuls in the stable before. I wouldn't know what to charge."

"It ought to be half. You won't have to curry or feed him. I'll pay double the regular rate. See Yardlinger for your money when he's on his feet."

The doctor hailed me. "I'll need help getting these men over to the Freestone. I can't treat them out here."

"Devil take the Freestone." Yardlinger gathered his legs under him, attempted to rise, lost his footing and slammed down on his tailbone with an impact that shook the saloon's porch. He blinked dazedly. A nervous titter rippled through the growing crowd.

"Concussion," said Ballard, adjusting the deputy's bandage. "Couple of days' rest will fix that up."

I designated a number of townsmen to help with the injured pair and started walking. I was striding as I turned onto Arapaho Street, my boots clomping on the boardwalk and echoing like shots in the porch rafters. People who had come out to see what was going on made way for me when they saw my face. Sensing excitement, some of them followed me, and then some more, so that by the time I reached Martha's place I was heading a motley parade. On the strip of grass that separated the house from the street I turned around, glaring. They stopped and I mounted the steps to the door alone.

The door crashed against the wall as I went through it

without knocking. A vase of flowers fell from a window sill and broke, water darkening the floral print carpet. An over-ripe blonde in a thin cotton shift threw me a startled glance from the settee. Her eyes traveled over me, and then she smiled, fingering back a stray tendril of yellow hair gray at the roots. She had freckles on her teeth like an old horse. Seated next to her, a thickset man in a prickly suit and a paper collar too small for his bull neck started to rise, then sat back down. He had a tea cup and saucer balanced on one knee and his lips were pursed under a bristling moustache. I recognized him as the town barber and a member of the city council.

"Evening, Marshal." He transferred the crockery from his knee to the arm of the settee. It rattled slightly. "What was all the shooting about? This young lady was kind enough to invite me in out of the line of fire."

I wasn't paying attention to him. Martha was standing before the beaded doorway leading into the next room, all six feet of her, the good eye cocked in my direction. "Where's Colleen?" I demanded.

She said, "This carpet was woven in Asia two hundred years before I was born. If you've stained it—"

I repeated the question, advancing on her. She placed a hand over the brooch at her neck. Another woman might have swooned or begun screaming. "Upstairs. First door on the left." She moved away from the opening.

I dashed aside the beads, found the staircase, and vaulted up two steps at a time. The door was locked. It flew open on the second kick, overturning a pedestal table and an earthenware pot containing a fern whose fronds hung to the floor. My heels ground the spilled black dirt into the rug. I'd graduated from horses to plants.

"Who the hell do you think you are?"

She stood next to a vanity, wearing a thin flannel nightgown and holding a tortoiseshell brush. Her red-brown hair flowed loose over her shoulders, glowing in the lamplight from the fresh stroking.

My anger had been building from the moment I'd exposed the Six Bar Six brand on the dead horse's flank. Face to face with its source, my rage leveled off. I closed the door almost gently and stood with my back to it.

"Nice touch, brushing your hair," I said. "Salome danced."

Something fluttered over her face, I couldn't tell what. When she spoke again her voice was no longer shrill. "What are you talking about? What was happening downtown? I heard the shooting. I thought some cowhands were blowing off steam." Fear gripped her then, draining the color from her features. "Why is your face black?" It was almost a whisper.

"Who'd you take up with?" I said calmly. "Mather or Turk? Whose idea was it to tell me that Mather was hitting Terwilliger in the morning so that I wouldn't expect him to attack me tonight? Pick one or all three. Just give me an answer."

Her fingers went to her mouth in admirably feigned fright. If it was feigned. I was in no condition to judge. "I didn't know." This time I barely heard it.

I didn't say anything. I hadn't the faintest notion of what to say or do. What had I been thinking all the way there? It angered me that she wasn't a man, and it angered me that that angered me. A few years earlier I'd have shot her where she stood without regard to her sex, but that was before the dime novels came and ruined me along with every other Westerner who read one just because there was nothing else to do in the middle of all that emptiness. Life was hard enough on the frontier without having to conform to a creed. I started to leave.

"You're not hurt." She was barefoot and made no noise hurrying across the rug. The top of her head barely reached my chin. Her hands grasped my shoulders. Tiny hands. It was hard to imagine them palming an ace. Her hair smelled of the scented soap they used downstairs, and something else.

I might have been gnarled wood in her hands for all the response she got. "One of my deputies is down with what might be a cracked skull," I said quietly. "The other one may lose his arm and probably his life. Me? I'm indestructible."

Her nails dug into my skin. "It wasn't a lie, Page. I did hear them planning to raid the Circle T. They didn't say anything about attacking you. They didn't. I'd have told you if they did." The gold flecks swirled in her eyes.

I shook off her hands and grasped her wrists. I could have broken them both with little effort.

"Maybe you weren't lying. Maybe Mather's men knew I depended on Martha for information and spread that story knowing it would reach me sooner or later and put me off guard when they hit town. But I can't chance it, understand? I can't chance it."

She grimaced. I was hurting her wrists. I slackened my hold. The smell of her made my head swim.

"I'd never be able to relax with you," I continued. "I couldn't hold you without wondering if you were signaling someone over my shoulder. We couldn't go riding but that I'd think you had a sniper laying for me along the road. It wouldn't last a week, and when it was over we'd carry away the bitter taste."

She lowered her eyes. I released her wrists and she turned away. Then she faced me again, across a distance of four feet.

"When I was three years old my father took me from Ohio down to the Nations and married a Cherokee woman for her land," she said huskily. "He called himself a farmer, but he spent most of his time gambling at the trading post. At night he'd teach me to play poker, and when the other players complained about his dealing he'd have me sit in for him. At thirteen I could shave an ace in full view of a roomful of people and no one would notice. A year later my father sold me to a whiskey peddler named Bower for his route and a four-horse team.

"The reason Bower got rid of his route was he was his own best customer. He went crazy when he was drunk, and since I was always close by, he'd beat me until his arms got tired. One night after he'd done an especially good job of bloodying me I waited until he was snoring face down in the back of our wagon, and then I dug his Dragoon Colt from under a feed sack and emptied it into his back. I went clear around the cylinder and squeezed the trigger three times on empty chambers."

Lamplight haloed her head and painted shadows in the folds of her nightgown. With her hair loose and her feet bare, she looked like the thirteen-year-old girl she was talking about.

"He had three hundred dollars in gold in a strongbox," she went on. "I grabbed it, put on his riding clothes, unhitched a horse from the team and lit out. No one ever came after me. I don't think anyone much cared who had killed him as long as he was dead. When I got to Arkansas I invested in a new wardrobe and a finishing course in Little Rock. I was young, but I knew that without an education I'd never do better than Bower for a husband.

"I soon learned that rich husbands were out unless your family was old and established, and mine stopped at an unmarked grave outside Muskogee where they buried my father after he was murdered by a drunken Osage. So I came back to Miss Jessup's School for Genteel Young Ladies and took a job teaching. For a year I helped mold a dozen little Colleen Bowers until I couldn't stand it any more and left. By the time anyone missed me, I was twenty miles inside the Nations. *I was seventeen years old.*"

Someone was calling my name on Pawnee Street. It sounded like Cross, back from the Circle T. I heard horses outside, a lot of them. "Why tell me?" I asked her.

"Can't you see I'm sick to death of crime and treachery? Are your instincts so deep you can't put them behind you long enough to believe that? What else do I have to do to buy your trust?" Her hands were curled into tight little fists in front of her.

"I don't know." I fished for words. "I don't know that it can be bought. If I were a bootmaker or a farmer or even a whiskey peddler in the Nations, it might be for sale. But I'm not and it's not. The price is too high. I wish it weren't."

"It doesn't have to be." Her eyes were shining in the darkness on her face. "You don't have to stay a lawman."

I opened my mouth. I almost agreed. Then I remembered the two dead half-breeds in Yankton and wondered if they'd heard this speech. I closed it. "I'm sorry it didn't work out." I pulled open the door.

She might have said, "So am I." I couldn't be sure. The door closed on whatever she did say.

CHAPTER 21

Randy Cross met me coming around the corner from Arapaho Street. Beyond him, the main four corners were a jam of men and horses. Light from the windows slid along the oily barrels of rifles and shotguns and sparkled off modest raiments. Metal rattled, leather creaked, animals snuffed and blew. Steam curled around the mounts' fidgety legs like locomotive exhaust. Some of the men were carrying torches, and black smoke columned up from the flames and merged with the darkness above. The scene smelled of tobacco and burning pitch and sardines. A number of the volunteers had filled their pockets with stores in anticipation of a long ride.

"I been looking all over for you," complained the deputy. The ride to the ranch and back had sobered him. "I got your posse."

"So I see. How many?"

"Fourteen's all I can spare." The stout man I had seen at the Pardees' funeral called down from his perch astride a big sorrel. The brim of his slouch hat touched the hook of his nose and he was huddled in a coarse woolen overcoat cut for a much larger man, the sleeves turned back and the tails spread to cover his saddle. His stirrups were adjusted as high as they would go to accommodate his short legs.

"Who's running the ranch, Mr. Terwilliger?" I asked.

His fierce eyes smoldered in the shadows. "It was your business, maybe I'd say." He had a thin voice for his build, and his tone was Midwestern flat. "You're Murdock? You know none of this'd be necessary, you let Pardee treat with Mather when he wanted to."

"I'm not so sure Mather was behind the raid. Or the lynching."

"You got a dead horse with the Six Bar Six brand. What more you need?" His nervous excitement passed to his horse, which scooped its neck and danced from side to side. The rancher seemed to be holding the animal in check by no other means than sheer force of presence.

"May I speak to your men?" I asked him.

He took a beat to consider, then nodded abruptly. In my absence Cross had saddled and bridled my roan and brought it from the livery to hitch to the riddled rail in front of the Pick Handle. I slipped its tether and mounted, then trotted out in front of the others. They had been conversing among themselves in growls, but lapsed into silence when I appeared. I pinned on the star.

"This isn't a vigilante raid," I announced, after introducing myself to a chorus of muttered obscenities. "You're to be sworn in as special deputies. That means you'll take my orders and no one else's. It doesn't give you leave to commit murder. We'll fire if fired upon, but if not, we'll give the men we're after a chance to surrender before we start busting caps. Who objects to that?"

"Me." This from a lean horseman near the center, with cracks for eyes and a trailing moustache that completed the oriental effect. "Why should they get any more chance than they gave Dale Pardee?"

Agreement rumbled through the group.

"Ain't you the one killed our foreman?" challenged a voice from the rear. The rumbling grew loud. I urged the roan forward into the flickering torchlight. The noise died.

I addressed myself to the oriental-looking cowhand, whom I had picked out as the spokesman for the group.

"Pardee gave me the same treatment his brother got. I'm not his brother."

He said nothing. I raised my voice to take in the group. "I was told when I came here you wanted law. You don't get it by trampling over it when it doesn't suit you. Any man not in agreement with that is free to leave. If you decide to stick, I'll make holes in the first man who goes against me."

"Whose law is that?"

A new voice, deep in the assembly. I couldn't locate the owner.

"Mine." The roan started fiddle-footing. I squeezed my thighs together and it settled down. "One thing more. There's reason to believe Abel Turk is leading these night riders, not Mather. For sure Turk's with them. I know an experienced gunman when I see one, and it's only safe to assume he's surrounded himself with others as good. If that bothers you, go now. No one will think poor of you."

I stopped talking. The riders stirred, spoke to each other in murmurs that rose and died like sounds coming from a crowded room as a door swung open and shut.

"You sure Turk's part of it?"

The question had come from the porch of the Breen House, where a lanky figure was outlined dimly between the lighted windows. I couldn't make him out but I knew Shedwell's brogue.

"Fairly," I said. "Why?"

He stepped forward. His coattails were flung back to expose his guns. "I'll be one of your deputies. Unless you got objections."

Some of Terwilliger's crew recognized the mankiller. His name buzzed through the gathering.

"Get your horse," I told him.

He struck off toward the livery, moving with an easy lope. "What about it?" I asked the others. "Any dropouts?"

Terwilliger kneed his horse into the space in front of the

cowhands, facing me. "My men don't shy from a fight, Marshal. Swear away."

When Shedwell returned straddling a bay stallion, I had everyone raise his right hand and recite the oath I'd heard often in Judge Blackthorne's chambers when new officers joined the fraternity. The words didn't vary a lot between the federal and local levels and didn't mean much of anything anyway. After the "I do's" I said, "Kill the torches. No sense advertising," and led the way in the direction of the night riders' retreat. The dead raider had been removed from the street, which explained the light in Fitch's undertaking parlor.

We made good time until we reached the point where our quarry had left the road to ride across country, after which we had to stop from time to time and dismount until someone picked up on matted grass or a similar sign of recent passage. Moonlight is deceptive. We wasted precious minutes following false trails that dead-ended where the fugitives had doubled back on themselves to throw us off. Finally we came to a spot where the tracks stopped heading north and turned east.

"That ain't the way to Mather's spread," Terwilliger reported.

"Could be another sour lead," suggested Cross.

"I doubt it." I pointed to a spattering of dark spots on the beaten grass. "Whoever's bleeding has been doing it for miles. They're running out of time for clever tricks."

"How many of them are there, you reckon?" asked the rancher.

"Shedwell got the best look at them," I said.

"Eight." The gunman looked thoughtful. "Nine. I was sort of preoccupied."

I frowned. "Looked like more."

"Could be. Like I said, I didn't keep no tally."

"Think Périgueux knows they're on his land?" Terwilliger asked.

"It wouldn't surprise me." I clucked the roan into motion.

Half a mile farther on we came upon a bundle of clothing dumped alongside the trail. The horses were downwind of it and shied as we approached. It wasn't a bundle of clothing. I stepped down and turned it over with my foot.

The front of his shirt was black and glistening in the pale light. An empty scabbard like the kind cavalry officers wore was hooked to his belt. I remembered Major Brody saying he'd gutshot the man who had tried to lop off his arm. He wasn't wearing a pillowcase now. I recognized him as one of the men I had seen at the corral near Périgueux's headquarters. I felt his neck.

"Still warm," I said, mounting. "We're gaining."

An hour later we topped a rise overlooking several sections of undulating grassland. Nestled in a furrow between swells was a wooden line shack with a slant roof and a covered window with a gunport where the shutters met, left over from the Sioux wars. A brush tail flicked into view from beneath the roof of the lean-to stable in back and was gone. We withdrew below the ridge.

"Might be a decoy," Cross whispered. "They got a horse to spare now."

"If they've got wounded, they'll need shelter," I said.

"If they got wounded."

I considered. "I'm betting on the shack, but let's make sure. Circle around on foot. Stay low. If there's only one horse in the stable, fire a shot in the air and wait for us. Otherwise come back and report. Just a second."

The deputy had started off in a crouch. I clutched his sleeve. "If you start anything without orders, I'll kill you."

His eyes glittered in their slits but he said nothing. I let him go.

The rest of us stood around listening to each other's breathing. The prairie wind came up at ragged intervals, humming through the grass and plucking at our hat brims so that we had to hold on to them with both hands, but for the most part nothing moved. Even the moon seemed nailed in the sky. At last we heard Cross' heavy footsteps in the frost-brittle grass.

"There's nine horses." His breath came in shallow, excited bursts.

"Fan out," I said. "Surround it. No one fires till I give the word."

Cow horses all, the animals held their positions from the moment the reins touched earth. I kept Shedwell with me and divided the men between Cross and Terwilliger, thus balancing the command. When we were alone, the gunman and I crawled to the crest on our bellies. I had the Winchester from the office, he a Spencer repeater with a folding sight. I noted the moon's position.

"Sun will be up in about an hour. We'll call them out as soon as it gets light."

He made no reply. In the hollow, the lonely shack cast a shadow solid enough to trip over. Miles away a coyote hurled its sad challenge at the moon.

I blew on my fingers and worked the stiffness out of the joints. "Where do you know Abel Turk from?"

"Centralia, eighteen sixty-four." He was watching the shack.

"You were riding with Quantrill then."

"Anderson."

"Was Turk a guerrilla?"

"He was second in command." His voice was low. "We'd been picking Centralia all morning and was feeling pretty good. Along about noon we stopped the train from St. Charles and ordered everybody out. There was twenty-five armed Yanks aboard, going home on furlough. We lined them up and made them strip to their flannels. Anderson found out one was an officer and ordered him out of line. Then he told Turk to muster out the rest."

The broad brim of his hat drenched his face in darkness. His breath curled in the brittle air.

"I was pretty fresh then," he said. "I thought that meant Anderson was going to turn them loose. I laughed to think of all them bluebellies hobbling down the tracks in their long-handles and stocking feet. Then he started shooting at them.

"He blasted away with a pistol in each hand, and Yanks fell like dominoes. Some of them tried running and went down with holes in back. One blubbered and stuck out his hands like he thought he could stop the lead. There was this yellow-haired sergeant that let out a roar and charged Turk when he was reloading. Turk didn't hurry. He finished and shot the sergeant twice in the chest and once in the neck, and even then he had to step back or the Yank would of fell into his arms.

"By this time we was all shooting, me included. It wasn't hard at all. You'd be surprised how easy it was when everyone else was doing it too. Thing is, I don't think any of us could of touched it off except Turk. When it was over, the only Yank left standing was the brass-buttons Anderson took out of line."

He chuckled dryly. "Old Bloody Bill, he did hold a soft spot for brother officers."

We listened to the coyote again, farther away this time, the mournful note warped by distance. When it had ended I said, "Is Turk the reason you came to Breen?"

He didn't answer. We waited in silence for the sun.

CHAPTER 22

It's quiet at that time of year, with no crickets singing or bugs thumping through the grass. We lay there watching the shack while the cold sniffed at us and crept down our collars and up our pants legs and lay like metal against our skin. Even the faraway coyote had ceased crying. I warmed my hands in my armpits and creaked my toes in my boots when they grew numb. The grass crackled when I changed positions. Shedwell didn't move a hair.

For a long time I watched a leaden sliver on the eastern horizon before it lost its hard edge and melted into the black that surrounded it, spreading with the painful slowness of a bad dream drawing to a close. The sky bled gray, then pale blue, and then a wedge of red sun appeared like a raw wound in the Little Belts. The shadow cast by the line shack shifted and shortened, becoming more dramatic as coppery light washed the foothills.

I waited while the sun cleared the mountains and its glare grew less direct. Then I gathered my legs beneath me and, squatting on one knee, drew a bead on the shuttered window. Beside me, Shedwell remained prone, supported on his elbows, with the Spencer trained on the door.

My own voice surprised me, booming out over the hills after so much silence and bounding off the tall rocks to east and west. "Surrender" continued to ricochet long after I finished speaking, altering its shape each time it struck until it was just a grumble in the distance, then a whisper, then nothing. More minutes passed before my answer came screaming straight at me and buried itself with a *whump* in the earth at my feet. Blue smoke slid sideways from the port in the shutters.

"Open fire!" On "fire" I squeezed one off, levering another into the chamber and shooting again even as the silvery tinkle of collapsing glass reached me. The door jumped in its frame as Shedwell's bullet smashed through the weathered wood.

Reports crackled across the surrounding hills. Balls of smoke were blown elliptical and shredded by the mounting wind. Pieces of shingle flew from the shack's roof. Lead whined off solid objects inside and clanked against ironware. The horses in the exposed stable screamed and kicked at the posts supporting the roof, the impacts sounding like small explosions even at this distance.

The men trapped inside returned fire sporadically. A black snout would poke itself through the port, sneeze fire and smoke, then withdraw as more bullets chewed at the shutters. Reports from the opposite side testified to the existence of at least one other window. Meanwhile, hurtling bits of metal hammered the weatherboard. I remember thinking of a magician I had once seen in St. Louis who shut a pretty girl up in a box and proceeded to thrust swords through the sides at all angles, and I wondered now, as I had wondered then, how anyone could survive such an assault. But the answering fire continued.

I was reloading when the shutters and door burst outward simultaneously as if a powder charge had gone off inside. Four men spilled out, arms and legs uncoiling like loosely baled rags as they struck the ground and straightened running, revolvers and rifles blazing. Bullets tore up grass all around me.

The one who had come through the door, working the lever of a Henry now and backing with the others toward the stable, wore a dark beard. Turk. Shedwell recognized him too, but before he could take aim the earth heaved in front of his face, spraying dirt into his eyes. He cursed and rubbed at them with his fingers.

I chambered a cartridge and got a bead on Turk just as he darted around the corner of the shack. My bullet splintered wood. One of the men who had leaped out the window was down, spread-eagled on his stomach with his six-gun still in his hand. Seconds later two horses bolted from the stable, their riders hugging their necks bareback. I fired and one horse went down with a scream. Its master leaped clear. It was Turk again.

I had him in my sights when his partner swung his horse around and crossed in front to give him a hand up. Someone on the other side squeezed off at the same time I did. The rider arched his back and slumped forward. Turk pushed him off and mounted in the same movement. He was a hundred yards away before his rescuer stopped bouncing. Dark geysers erupted around horse and rider. They disappeared over a hill, and when they came into view again atop the next they were well out of range. A number of desultory shots were hurled after them nonetheless.

Then it got quiet.

I waited for the appearance of the fourth escapee. When he didn't show I assumed one of the others had gotten him. I learned later that the others were thinking the same thing on our side. The missing man would be found draped over the hitching rail, where he had succumbed to a wound suffered while still in the building.

I asked Shedwell about his eyes, red-rimmed now and blinking. He waved the question aside.

"Turk get clear?"

I said he had. "He'll head toward Périgueux's for supplies and a fresh mount. It's closer than Mather's house."

"Don't shoot!"

The shout came from the shack, where moments later a rifle

and two revolvers flew out the open door in order and landed on the ground twenty feet away.

"We're unarmed!" The voice was hoarse and desperate. "We're coming out!"

"Hands on your heads!" I shouted.

I gave the order to cease fire. Two men staggered out the door one after the other, hands clasped on top of their heads. The second man was limping. Blood slicked his right pants leg to the knee. I called for them to halt and stood up. Brass casings tinkled from my lap to the ground.

"What about the others?" I kept them covered.

The uninjured man answered. His hair and short beard were snarled as if he'd just risen from bed.

"One's dead. The other, almost. He got it in the lungs and he's coughing up bloody pieces. That's it."

I called for Cross. There was a pause while his name banged around the mountains, and then a solid figure rose from the ridge on the other side of the shack. He waved the Spencer he'd taken from the rack at the jail and started down the slope. Terwilliger and his men followed suit. I was waiting for them when they got to the building, having taken possession of the prisoners and their discarded weapons. As he was closing in, Cross pivoted suddenly and smashed his rifle stock across the wounded man's face.

I dropped the confiscated guns and lashed out even as the man fell, catching the deputy full on the chin with my left fist. This was the same hand I had used to silence Colleen and Earl. I felt tiny bones snapping when it connected. My bones.

He staggered back a dozen steps, roared, and brought up the office Spencer. I sailed a bullet past his ear from the Winchester before he could pull the trigger.

"I don't miss twice," I barked, when it looked as if he was going to try again. He dropped his arm. Blood trickled out a corner of his mouth. I turned to Shedwell. "Can you handle things here?"

"You handle them," he said. "My business is with Turk."

Terwilliger was roughly helping Cross's victim to his feet. The night rider's nose was broken and bleeding copiously. "You're in charge," I told the rancher. "Try and see that no one gets lynched while we're gone."

The sun was clear of the peaks and losing its bloody color when Shedwell and I rode within view of the massive skeleton of the Marquis' new chateau. The numbness had worn out of my left hand, and each time the roan lurched, tiny bursts of pain shot straight up my arm. In spite of this we drove our mounts hard for the next half hour and thundered into Périgueux's yard just as Turk was emerging from the ranch house.

In his arms he cradled a bedroll bulky with foodstuffs. A sleek dun was ground-tethered by the corral, saddled and ready to run. We drew our revolvers and fired over its head. It whinnied, reared and took off at a mad gallop toward the hills, reins flapping.

Turk dropped his bundle and answered with his Smith & Wesson, backing away fast. I'd never seen anyone get a gun out that quickly. A furrow appeared across the horn of my saddle, exposing dull lead under the leather. Shedwell circled to the end of the porch and whipped his horse up onto the boards, ducking to clear the roof and block that line of retreat. We had him between us now.

The foreman sank into a half-crouch, swinging his gun to cover us both as he backed toward the corner of the house. I danced the roan in that direction, herding him in the other direction like a contrary bull.

My hat was snatched off my head by a bellowing explosion from above. Startled, I glanced up and met Ed Strayhorn's gaze at an upstairs window, behind the sight of his big Remington rifle. I'd completely forgotten about Périgueux's bookkeeper. I snapped off a hasty shot before he could take aim again. He ducked behind the wall and the window frame splintered.

A battering ram struck my chest. My horse reared and I cartwheeled from the saddle, turned over with agonizing slowness as in a terrifying dream, and stopped suddenly with an impact that dwarfed the first. What breath I still had left me with an animal grunt.

When my senses returned I raised my head to look for my horse and pain tore through me. I laid it back down, but not before noting that my shirt front was clotted with gore. I knew I was dying. I had seen what a bullet from a .44 could do to bone and muscle too many times to believe otherwise. Vaguely, not too far away, I heard a series of reports, a pause, and then one more. The last one carried the finality of an exclamation point. I remember thinking that that was important, then reminding myself that it wasn't, not any more, not to me. I could hear the squishy sound of blood pumping through the hole in my chest.

I may have blacked out. In any case, I don't recall any other thoughts until I heard a crunching and Chris Shedwell moved into my field of vision. His expression was grim and he was plodding like a man in the final stages of exhaustion. His right arm hung limp at his side with the Remington revolver dangling at the end. His other hand was clasped to his rib cage, where a red stain was spreading around his fingers. He stopped, looking down at me, and opened his mouth to speak.

A shot rang out, very close. His mouth opened a little wider along with his eyes. For a long moment he remained like that, back arched, elbows drawn in, and then the gun dropped from his hand, his knees buckled, and he fell out of my line of sight. Behind where he had been standing I now saw young Arnie Strayhorn holding the rifle his father had taken from him until he could show he deserved to carry it. The last thing I was aware of was his thin, bespectacled face wreathed in blue smoke.

CHAPTER 23

I dreamed of naked women and oceans of blood, of diabolic, laughing faces erupting from the muzzles of guns and scaly hands slippery to the touch that grasped my limbs in grips like steel cables and strained to pull me apart. One of the laughing faces belonged to Doc Ballard. The hands belonged to Alf, the bartender at the Glory. The blood was mine and so were the naked women, dredged up from my imagination and forgotten since I was fourteen years old. From time to time I'd see a man strapped to a bed and raving. I felt sorry for him, and sympathetic tears would roll down my cheeks and leave burning furrows. I found myself dreaming of him more and more often. He wasn't raving any more and the straps were gone.

"Murdock?"

It was the first time I'd heard human speech in my dreams. I strained to understand what was being said.

"Murdock? Wake up."

My eyelids were weighted at the bottoms, like curtains on a saloon stage. When I got them pried open, I was looking through a red haze. I closed them again and opened them. Again. The haze dissipated slowly, like frost on the inside of a window as a room warms up. The doctor's face hovered over me. He wasn't laughing.

"I've been having some crazy dreams." It came out gibberish. I started again, but he'd understood.

"That was the laudanum. You've been out for six days. You

were feverish when Terwilliger's men brought you in. I didn't dare drug you until it broke. I had to get someone to hold you down when I extracted the bullet. You screamed bloody murder."

"Alf?"

He looked surprised. "Yes, it was Alf. I didn't think you'd remember. The Glory had the nearest bed. That's where you are now, in the back room. You were delirious for days; I didn't think we'd pull you through."

I glanced down at my chest. I was shirtless. A white bandage swaddled my right shoulder above a coarse gray blanket.

"You took a bullet in the chest," he explained. "It just missed your right lung." He held up a conical lump of dull metal. "You were lucky twice. Ordinarily the lead would have pierced the lung, glanced off the shoulder blade, and torn a path through your vital organs before coming to rest. In this case it entered at an upward angle, scraped along the bone and became entangled in the muscles and ligaments of your shoulder. There was substantial tissue damage. You may lose some of the use of that arm. It's too early to tell. But it beats dying."

I lifted my left arm. My fingers protruded from a plaster cast that reached to my wrist. Cross's jaw had been harder than expected. The doctor smiled.

"When you decide to hurt yourself, you don't stop halfway. It'll take six weeks for those bones to finish knitting, but you can write and feed yourself."

"When can I get out of here?"

"Whenever you want to. But you won't want to for a while. You lost a lot of blood and you don't take too well to being fed, as this eye can attest." He indicated his left eye. It did look a little discolored and puffy.

"Shedwell," I said.

He looked grave. "There was nothing anyone could do for him. He died instantly." He paused. "Major Brody is gone too. He lived for a day after his arm was amputated, but the shock was just too much for his heart. He had an attack a couple of years ago. I guess you didn't know that."

I said I didn't. His manner lightened.

"You have a visitor. Shall I show him in?"

I don't remember how I answered. I must have said yes, because he went out and a moment later Yardlinger appeared at the foot of the bed. He was carrying his hat and had a patch over his eyebrow. I levered myself into a sitting position, stifling an exclamation as pain streaked down my weakened right arm.

"How's the head?" I asked.

"Stuck together with crepe and spit." He fingered the patch. "I won't be as pretty as I used to be, but few people are. How's the shoulder?"

"Ask me again when the laudanum wears off. I'm sorry about the Major. For a bloodthirsty guerrilla he had the makings of a first-class lawman."

He smiled wearily. "Just as well he didn't live to hear that. You know you left me in the lurch. Randy and I have had the devil's own time keeping our prisoners from being lynched. We had to club a couple of heads last night, but it looks as if they'll live long enough to face the circuit judge this afternoon."

"Who've we got?"

"Well, Périgueux's the star. It was his idea to form the band of night riders. The two survivors have confirmed that and we've got Mather's testimony that he sold a string of black horses to the Marquis a month before the raids started. He suspected the Frenchman was involved but was afraid those horses would implicate him so he kept quiet. I'm convinced he wasn't in on the raids and that he didn't know his own foreman was leading them. If he's guilty of anything, it's being afraid to ask questions."

"Where's Périgueux now?"

"Terwilliger's men are guarding him at his place. They're still sworn and they know what's in store for them if anything happens to their prisoner. The jail's at capacity."

"Who's there, besides the two night riders?"

"Actually, there's only one. Doc Ballard's treating his partner at the Freestone for a hip wound. Both the men who were still in the line shack were dead when Randy and the others found them. Three Circle T hands involved in the raid on Mather's ranch. The other two rode out that night. I don't have any evidence other than my testimony that they were with Pardee when his brother was brought into Fitch's, but I'm going with that. Then there's Ed Strayhorn and his nephew Arnie."

"They were with Turk?"

He shook his head. "The old man thought he was just protecting his boss's interests when the shooting started. I mean to put in a word for him at the trial. As for Arnie, well, I don't see him pulling much more than a suspended sentence considering Shedwell's reputation. The judge takes a dim view of professional killers."

I was having a hard time keeping up. The laudanum had dulled my comprehension. "What about Turk?"

"Terwilliger got there just in time to see it from a distance." He spoke slowly. "After he shot you, Turk took cover in what there was of Périgueux's new chateau. Shedwell went in after him standing up. The night rider wounded him first shot. From then on Shedwell might have been invisible the way Turk's bullets just kept stitching up the ground all around him. Shedwell fired once. Just once."

I considered. "Arnie must have seen it too. When he realized who it was, he must have gone to get the English rifle, thinking that killing Chris Shedwell would make him man enough for his uncle."

"Men have died for lots less," he said. "Anyway, Terwilliger's the one to thank for saving your hide. He threw you in one of the Marquis' wagons and trundled you into town more dead than alive."

"Damn nice of him, considering I saved him a few dead men himself. Any messages?"

"I almost forgot." He reached inside his coat and drew out a sheaf of telegraph forms. "Guess who."

"Answer them. Tell the Judge I'll report in person." I searched his face. "Anything else?"

"No word from her. She hasn't budged from Martha's since you were brought here." Angrily he thrust the forms back into his breast pocket. "She's no good, Page."

I laughed nastily. Even that hurt. "Who am I, the Pope?"

"You know what I mean."

The doctor returned. "That's enough visiting for now. He needs rest."

As he said it I realized how tired I really was. I held out my left hand. "I can't say you didn't keep me entertained."

Yardlinger grasped my fingers in the cast. "Don't worry about Doc's bill or the rent on this room. The city's taking care of it, though the council doesn't know that yet. Your horse is at the livery and I've got your gun. Anytime you're ready for them."

I grinned. "Marshal, are you ordering me out of town?"

"Maybe." His tight smile flickered behind the lank moustache. "The sooner you're gone the quicker I can get the citizens of Breen accustomed to orthodox law enforcement." He left. I was asleep before the door closed.

That afternoon I was walking around the room, and by the next day I could dress myself and venture out to the barroom for a beer and some conversation with Alf. There was no news from the new opera house, where the trial was in its second day. The bartender caught my attention wandering toward the deserted side room.

"She ain't been around," he said, polishing a glass. "Talk is she's leaving."

I paid for the beer without a word and returned to the back room. My shoulder was beginning to act up in spite of the sling.

The trial lasted three days. Michel d'Oléron, Marquis de Périgueux, was found guilty of conspiracy to commit murder and sentenced to life imprisonment. He never spent a day behind bars. The sentence was later commuted to ten to twenty years at hard labor, then suspended. He sold out his holdings in Montana and returned to France, where rumor had it that he married into another fortune after his first wife, a woman of frail constitution, perished during the ocean crossing. The two night riders were hanged in Breen for murder. The jury found Ed Strayhorn innocent of complicity in the raids and he was released. His nephew Arnie received six months on a work detail clearing land for the Great Northern Railroad, scheduled for completion in 1883. After that he joined a theatrical troupe and toured some eastern cities as "The Man Who Shot Chris Shedwell." I lost track of him in succeeding years.

In a separate action, the circuit judge dismissed out of hand the case against the three Terwilliger men for lack of evidence. No one ever came to trial for the raid on the Six Bar Six and the murder of three employees of the ranch.

Dick Mather died of consumptive bronchitis in 1882.

By a six-to-four vote of the city council, Oren Yardlinger was appointed to a two-year term as Breen city marshal. The appointment wasn't renewed and he drifted down to Wyoming, where he took a job as deputy sheriff in Cheyenne and was shot in the back by an unknown party while making his rounds. He died with his Navy Colt still in its holster. I didn't hear of Randy Cross again until 1899, when he refereed the Jeffries-Fitzsimmons fight in Coney Island, N.Y. After that, nothing.

The last I heard, Bob Terwilliger was still alive and living in comfortable retirement on his ranch, now under the management of his son.

Against doctor's orders I testified on the last day of the night-rider trial and retired to the Glory during the recess for a drink. Colleen Bower was in the side room, dealing blackjack to a man in a suit with an eastern cut.

I peeled enough off the roll Yardlinger had returned to me for my bills at the hotel and livery, bought some chips out of the rest, and slapped what was left down on the table in front of the easterner. "Try your luck at the wheel."

He glanced up, annoyed. Then he saw the sling I was wearing and went a little pale. He scooped up the bills and his chips, mumbled polite excuses to the lady, and went out. My reputation was spreading.

"Any news?" She dealt two cards apiece without looking at me. Her hair was done up the way I liked it and she was wearing blue.

"Judge turned it over to the jury. Nothing to do now but wait. Twenty-one." I turned up the ace of hearts.

"Twenty."

I took in her ante. She dealt again. "Been sick?" I asked.

"I needed a little vacation. Nineteen."

"Seventeen." I watched my chip go onto her stack and fed the pot again. "You knew Chris Shedwell pretty well, didn't you?"

She didn't answer. Cards slithered over the table's polished top. "I'm over."

I claimed her chip. "Well enough to scout for him, I'd say."

She hesitated, then resumed dealing. Her eyes never left the cards. I grabbed her hand. She glared.

"It was convenient for Shedwell," I said. "Not every killer has someone he can blame for his profession. He could fancy himself a soldier until that day in Centralia when Abel Turk made a murderer out of him and the others in Anderson's crew.

"Being confined to a bed gives you a chance to think. I kept wondering what it was that made Shedwell hate him enough to want to kill him. When he told me about Centralia I thought it was because of what Turk had done to those unarmed Union soldiers, but that wasn't it. It was because of what he thought Turk had done to him. It's been eating at him all this time. Maybe he thought destroying Turk would wipe out the last sixteen years and let him start over clean."

Still she didn't say anything. I held on. I knew from experience that she had to be a captive audience to listen.

"Then I started wondering how he found out Turk was here. That wasn't too hard to answer. You were the only person he knew in Breen. How did you send the wire, in code? Something you fixed up together before he sent you in this direction to nose around and find out what you could? It doesn't really matter how you did it. But it was smart. Who'd suspect a lady gambler of spying for a killer?"

She had a new handbag. I caught her eyes wandering toward it and released her hand to slide it toward me. It was heavier than most reticules. She sighed resignedly and sat back.

"It wasn't like that at all." One of her fine white hands went up before I could interrupt. "Oh, I sent him a wire, and I used a simple code designed to stand up to a first glance. But he didn't send me here. I recognized Turk by accident from Chris's description when Turk visited Martha's. Chris didn't depend on women to lay his groundwork. And he didn't come here to kill Turk. I thought you understood that."

I summoned a sneer. Then I spotted my reflection in the glass chimney of the lamp on the table and stopped. "He didn't go out to Périgueux's ranch to swap old war stories."

She shook her head, exasperated at my density. "I'm not saying Chris wouldn't have tried to kill him if he thought he could. He didn't think he was good enough. As it turned out he was, but he couldn't know that. He had nothing but memory to compare with."

I stared at her, trying to put what she said in order. This time I couldn't blame it on laudanum. "You're saying he came here to die."

"Is it so hard to accept?" She pushed aside the deck of cards. "Some people slash their wrists. Others take a gun and blow their brains out. Chris chose the way he thought was best for him. I like to think that Doc Ballard was wrong and that he had a chance to realize what had happened when that unexpected bullet hit him. That way he would've died content."

"He hated living that much?"

"Not living, waiting to die. Have you ever heard of the law of diminishing returns? They talk about it a lot back East. The more durable you make a product, the lower your chances of selling a replacement because the first one never wears out. When you're best, you sow the seeds of your own destruction. With Chris, it stood to reason that if he kept killing off the gunmen who weren't as good as he was, the odds of his meeting one as good or better increased. No, it wasn't living he hated. It was waiting."

I didn't say anything. After a few moments she retrieved the deck and dealt. We played a few hands, winning each other's money, then: "Alf tells me you're heading out."

"Soon as I can hire a wagon." She dealt herself twenty-one. "I don't need one, but a lady of my breeding can't be seen riding horseback across the prairie."

I won the next turn. "Ladies don't travel alone."

"Is that an invitation?"

"If you're headed west."

She shook her head. "If you can survive the Nations without an escort, you can survive anywhere." She won the last hand, drew in the discards and shuffled the deck. "Care for another go? Maybe we can break this deadlock."

"I wish we could." I got up, taking my chips. I started to say something else. She put more energy into her shuffling, the cards hissing. Her eyes remained on the deck. I moved toward the door.

"Planning to hang around Helena for a while?"

I stopped, my back to her. "For a while."

There was a pause, then: "Thanks for the warning."

I left. Outside, it was a bright spring day.